Lass and Found

Sandra Orchard

Annie's®
AnniesFiction.com

Books in the Scottish Bakehouse Mysteries series

Library of Congress-in-Publication Data
Lass and Found / by Sandra Orchard
p. cm.
I. Title
                        2019955597

AnniesFiction.com
(800) 282-6643
Scottish Bakehouse Mysteries™
Series Creator: Shari Lohner
Series Editor: Elizabeth Morrissey
Cover Illustrator: Kelley McMorris

10 11 12 13 14 | Printed in China | 9 8 7 6 5 4 3 2

1

At the tinkle of the bell on Bread on Arrival's front door, Carol MacCallan brushed flour off her hands, then tucked a wayward hank of silver-streaked hair back behind her ear before bustling from the commercial kitchen out to the front counter. The 55-year-old retired math teacher enjoyed helping customers when she got a chance, though managing accounts and baking special-order cakes comprised her primary duties. Fortunately, the talents of her co-owners, Laura Donovan and Molly Ferris, rounded out the bakery's management quite nicely.

Laura, former head chef of a NYC restaurant, took charge of creating most of their delicacies, especially developing new recipes that heralded the bakehouse's Scottish theme—a nod to the fierce Scottish pride of Loch Mallaig, the quaint and quirky village in Michigan's Upper Peninsula where the bakery resided. Both Laura and Carol happily left Bread on Arrival's marketing to their other former college roommate, Molly. After all, she was the mastermind behind the bakery's name, which honored the fact that it was housed in a former funeral parlor. Molly also handled front-of-house duties alongside two part-time staffers, retired history teacher Hamish Bruce and college student Bridget Ross . . . although none of them were present to help their first customer of the morning.

Carol welcomed Reverend Stuart Findlay with a smile. "*Guid mornin*, Reverend." She'd recently adopted the greeting in honor of her paternal grandparents, who hailed from Edinburgh and had always said good morning to her in the same way.

"Same to you, Carol." Reverend Findlay returned her smile, his dark eyes warm and twinkling. His gaze alighted on the display case of Scottish baked goods, and he clasped his hands enthusiastically. "And a good morning it is. I see you've got my favorite—blueberry scones."

"Made with berries my grandkids picked yesterday. Thankfully Maisie and Gavin didn't eat all of them before they brought me the spoils." Carol grabbed a bakery tissue from a nearby box. "Just one today?"

"Don't tell Bonnie, but make it two." The reverend wiggled his eyebrows. "I'm working with the kids in Vacation Bible School again this morning, and I need fortification. It's day four out of five."

"You certainly need plenty of energy for that." Carol grinned as she bagged the scones. "Especially since my daughter signed up the twins. I don't think seven-year-olds have an off button."

"I don't believe they do." Reverend Findlay chuckled as he pulled out his wallet. "Though Jenny and Craig seem to have taught them good manners." He paid for his purchase and left.

As the door swung shut behind the reverend, Carol caught sight of another familiar face. "It must be Thursday," she murmured as Jeanette Franklin—one of their regulars—bypassed the front door, her friendly spaniel, Scout, in tow. Carol knew she was heading around the house toward the fenced backyard, which the bakery staff cheekily referred to as "the barking lot." Customers were welcome to leave their well-behaved pets in the yard while they were inside.

Molly's Scottish terrier, Angus, who lived in the apartment upstairs with his mistress, considered it his calling to be a canine ambassador to four-legged guests and was usually on alert for visitors. At the sound of Angus catapulting out of his second-story dog door, Carol glanced through the side window as he scampered down the exterior stairs, yipping jubilantly. She went to the back entrance to let Jeanette in that way, which was more convenient.

Carol opened the door and peeked outside. "You can come through here, Jeanette."

"Just a sec." Jeanette attempted to untangle herself from Scout, who'd wound his leash around her in his excited reunion with Angus.

"Shush, Angus," Carol scolded mildly. She adored him, but she also knew Molly would give him the same rebuke if she were here instead of out on a delivery.

"He's fine." Jeanette latched the gate closed, then unsnapped the lead from her dog's collar. "Scout loves him."

A fit fortysomething, Jeanette struck Carol as the quintessential outdoorsy type, always in a plaid shirt, jeans, and hiking boots with a backpack slung over her shoulders. True to the common belief that dogs often resemble their owners, Scout not only shared Jeanette's love of hiking through the seemingly endless forests of the UP, but he also had remarkably similar close-set eyes flanking a narrow nose.

Carol watched the dogs sniff each other then give chase around the yard, tromping through the grass covered in cool dew that would soon evaporate into another warm July day. "They're settling in fine," she said. "Come on in. I'll get your order ready."

"Thanks." Jeanette shrugged her backpack from her shoulders as she followed Carol to the front of the bakery. "Your oatcakes have become a staple for our hikes."

Smiling, Carol began assembling a cardboard box to fill with Jeanette's standing order of four dozen sugar-free oatcakes.

"Hi, Mrs. Franklin. I already prepped your order," Bridget called from the eating area, where she was restocking sugar packets at the coffee doctoring station. She must have arrived and gotten to work in the short amount of time Carol had been outside. The Superior Bay College student was a remarkable self-starter and her striking hazel eyes, framed by stylishly bobbed black hair streaked with purple, never missed a thing. Bridget pointed to a taped box on the counter opposite the cash register.

Carol scooped up the box and handed it to Jeanette with a grin. "And they say you can't find good help these days." Carol shot a smile at Bridget, who'd thankfully been able to take on more hours for the busy summer months.

"It's true," Jeanette agreed. "My daughter's the same age as Bridget, and she's always complaining that her classmates don't want to work. At least not at their studies."

"Well, we've been blessed then." Carol's heart swelled as the truth of it sank in. The reality was they hadn't expected their online sales, especially of wedding cakes, to take off as quickly as they had. And with Loch Mallaig's bustling tourist season now in full swing, Bridget had become an indispensable part of their team.

Jeanette nodded. "We certainly have."

Carol rang up Jeanette's oatcakes on the cash register. "Will there be anything else today?"

"Hold on." Laura hurried out of the kitchen brandishing a huge tray of parlies, their fresh-baked ginger aroma filling the room. "Before you decide, you can be the first to sample today's special."

"I'm honored." Jeanette eyed Laura's tray. "What's the special?"

"This is pending Molly's approval, but . . ." Laura's brown eyes twinkled. "I'm thinking each day we'll offer a different kind of treat with a special deal. So for example, today all redheads, including those who are auburn like me"—Laura took a model's pose drawing their attention to her hair—"or who are ginger like you, get a special deal on parlies, or parliament cakes as they're formally known." Laura inhaled deeply. "Because, as you can smell, they are ginger cookies. And ginger is reddish. Get it? So redheads can buy six, get one free."

"Hey," Bridget said, her tone mock insulted. She flicked her dark, glossy hair, which was courtesy of her Chinese-American and Hispanic heritage. "What about the rest of us?"

"Your turn will come," Laura assured her. "Another day, we can offer black buns to customers with black hair."

Bridget wrinkled her nose. "Fruitcake?"

Laura bit her lip. "Well, maybe something with chocolate instead."

"You could give a deal on snowballs to people with white hair," Jeanette suggested.

"And chocolate chip cookies for those of us with salt-and-pepper locks," Carol chimed in, patting her own hair.

"Exactly," Laura said, her spirits seeming to lift once more.

Bridget twirled the purple streak decorating her hair. "How about Empire biscuits for those of us with purple streaks?" She had a special affection for the jam-filled sugar cookies decorated with icing.

"Sure," Laura agreed. "I'll figure out a unique cookie for each hair color."

A young man who'd slipped into the bakery at some point during their discussion piped up. "What's the special for guys like me?" He rubbed his palm over his shaved head.

"How about peanut butter balls?" Laura asked.

He made a show of thinking it over. "Rum balls would be better."

Laura laughed. "I could make those. Let me go check my recipes." She disappeared back to the kitchen.

"I love a deal and my daughter loves gingersnaps, so I'll take the special, Carol." Jeanette put her box of oatcakes in her backpack, then pulled out her wallet. "And . . ." She scanned the display cases. "I'll have some Selkirk bannock to eat here." She glanced down the hallway toward the back door. "Scout will be happy for the chance to enjoy an extended visit with Angus."

Carol collected Jeanette's payment, then handed her a tray with her breakfast order, which Jeanette carried to an empty table.

The bald man slipped a baseball cap on his head and ordered coffee and a cinnamon bagel to go. "Can't wait for the rum ball special," he called from the door as he exited.

Doreen Giobsan, the thirtysomething owner of the Thistle and That gift shop next door, gave him a curious look as she passed him in the doorway. "You have rum balls?" she asked Carol as she approached the register.

"Not yet." Carol explained Laura's new scheme.

Doreen patted her dark red bob. "And of course she started with a special for redheads because it covers three-quarters of our town." Her sky-blue eyes twinkled. "We Scots can't resist getting anything for free."

Carol grinned. Many of Loch Mallaig's townsfolk prided themselves on managing to trace their ancestry to Scottish roots—some to quite renowned historical figures. Whether true or not, the stories certainly enhanced the unique feel of the town.

Doreen perused the display cases. "Free or not, I can't say I fancy gingersnaps at the moment." Unlike Jeanette, who more or less stuck to the same order, Doreen preferred to mix things up, rarely choosing the same cookie two visits in a row.

"Then what can I get for you today?" Carol asked.

"I guess baking arsenic into Henry Roberts's next order of sultana cakes would be too much to ask?"

Carol didn't know whether to wince or chuckle. "What did Henry do?" The man was in his early sixties, so Carol doubted he and Doreen had had a romantic tiff.

"What hasn't he done?" Doreen huffed. "Ever since he bought and renamed Barb Nolan's antiques shop, all I hear from the summer tourists is The Artful Codger this, and The Artful Codger that. I'm telling you, the man is a right chancer. He is seriously poaching my customers. At this rate, I'll never be able to pay back my brother, Glenn, the money he lent me to do renovations on the shop." She shook her head. "Makes me long to go back to the wellness retreat I went to last fall. Real life is too stressful."

"But you sell gifts of every description, and nothing used," Carol said. "I wouldn't have thought there'd be much overlap, if any, between your merchandise and an antiques shop. Was there a problem when Barb ran it?"

"Everything was fine before Barb retired to Florida." Doreen huffed. "All I know is that business in July is usually a lot brisker than this. And according to the tourists who liberally rave about the new-and-improved antiques store, Henry's furniture prices are a steal. Has to make one wonder what he paid for his merchandise, don't you think?" The inflection in Doreen's tone made it clear she suspected Henry Roberts wasn't on the up-and-up. "I mean, how do you trust someone who calls himself the artful codger? You know it's an allusion to that thief character in *Oliver Twist*, right?"

"I'm sure it's meant to be ironic," Carol said.

Bridget caught Carol's eye and jerked her head toward the front window. Outside, Henry Roberts was crossing the street, heading toward the bakery.

Carol nodded to Bridget. Since moving to town, Henry had become a regular too, and Carol certainly didn't want him to walk in on Doreen gossiping about him. "I'm sure folks are simply excited about the novelty of Henry's products." Carol's gaze strayed to the door as it opened.

Doreen glanced over her shoulder and sniffed indignantly. But at least when she turned back to the counter, she lowered her voice. "Antiques are hardly novel. It's his prices."

Laura emerged from the kitchen carrying a tray of fresh Empire biscuits for the display case.

"Ooh." Doreen's eyes lit up and she pointed to the cookies. "What kind of jam is in those?"

"Raspberry," Laura answered as she rested the tray on the counter.

"Yum. I'll take three dozen." Doreen's lips quirked into a satisfied smile. "They should entice the tourists to browse a little longer in my shop."

"Good thinking." Carol quickly assembled a box and carefully set three dozen cookies inside, depleting the supply Laura had just brought out.

"Guess I'd better go make more," Laura said with a laugh, then took the empty tray back to the kitchen.

As Carol rang up the order, Doreen turned to Henry. "Another beautiful shopping day ahead of us, wouldn't you say, Mr. Roberts?"

"Indeed, Miss Giobsan," he agreed, in the warm, resonant tone Laura had dubbed a radio voice.

Admirably, Doreen's cheery greeting didn't betray a shred of her misgivings about the man and his shop. Pulling out her wallet, Doreen said to Carol, "I'll take a cranachan and coffee with that too. For here. I skipped breakfast this morning."

Carol suppressed a smile. Ordering a light breakfast like the cranachan—a cream, oats, and fruit trifle—wasn't unusual for Doreen, but Carol couldn't help but think the gift shop owner wanted to stick around the bakery to spy on Henry.

"Let me carry that to a table for you," Bridget offered as Doreen juggled getting her wallet back in her purse while simultaneously reaching for the box of cookies and her breakfast tray.

"You're so sweet. Thank you." Her box of cookies in hand, Doreen trailed Bridget to the sitting area and stopped at the table closest to the counter. "Here is good," she called to Bridget, who'd already passed the table on her way to the more popular window seats.

The amused twinkle in Henry's eyes made Carol wonder if he too suspected Doreen's motive for the choice.

"A sultana cake?" Carol asked him.

"I've only been here a month and you already know me so well," Henry said, his sonorous voice lifting cheerily. "I'll have that, but I think Miss Giobsan is on to something. I'll take a couple dozen shortbread cookies as well."

Carol could almost hear a head of steam hissing from Doreen's direction.

Henry took his order to go and soon after he left the bakehouse, Doreen followed, clutching her box of customer-enticing Empire biscuits.

Jeanette, who'd lingered over her breakfast much longer than usual, approached Carol at the counter, visibly upset.

"Is there a problem with the bannock?" Carol glanced to where the woman had been sitting, but her plate and glass were empty.

"It's not that." Jeanette made a flustered gesture toward the door. "I couldn't help overhearing Doreen's speculation about Henry Roberts's antiques. I bought a beautiful coffee table from him earlier this week. Like she said, it was an amazing bargain. It has 'Made in Scotland 1908' wood burned on the underside, so I'm sure it's genuine. But . . ." Jeanette wrung her hands and nervously glanced around. "Does Doreen think his furniture is stolen?"

Carol shook her head. "I wouldn't worry if I were you. I imagine Doreen was speaking out of her own frustration with slumping sales and because her would-be customers all seem to be talking about Henry's unique offerings. I wouldn't put any stock in the speculation."

Jeanette nodded thoughtfully. "I'd hate to think I'd bought stolen property. You're probably right, but maybe I'll ask her about it the next time I see her." She said goodbye, then hurried toward the back door to retrieve Scout.

Molly entered the bakery through the rear entrance a few moments after Jeanette left through it. Holding Angus snugly in her arms, she walked to the front counter. "Jeanette seems quiet this morning," she said to Carol.

"She's just a little worried her new table from The Artful Codger is stolen," Carol said, then recapped the suspicions Jeanette had overheard Doreen share.

Molly grinned. "If he's got such good deals, maybe I ought to go shopping. I was thinking we need an accent table in the corner with the fireplace."

Carol raised an eyebrow. "I'm not sure scoring a deal from Henry is worth raising Doreen's ire. Then again . . ." She glanced toward the spot Molly had mentioned. "A little table might look nice there."

Just before closing time the following Wednesday afternoon, Molly and Carol were busily serving a sudden rush of customers when a college-age girl burst into the shop and frantically glanced around, her eyes red-rimmed and her mouse-brown pixie cut quite unkempt. Although she seemed vaguely familiar, Carol couldn't place her.

The girl spotted Bridget clearing tables and made a beeline her way. "Bridget!" she cried. "Something's happened to my mom. And the police won't do anything."

Startled at the girl's outburst, Bridget almost spilled the dishes precariously stacked on her tray. She set it on the table she'd just cleared. "What are you talking about, Annemarie? What happened?"

Carol mulled over the name. She didn't recognize it, but the petite girl was clearly a friend of Bridget's.

Twisting a sheet of paper in her hands, Annemarie's gaze darted around at the handful of customers staring her way as if also waiting to hear her answer. She smoothed out the paper and then hurried from table to table, asking each customer, "Have you seen this woman today?"

Some, like Doreen Giobsan's older brother, Glenn, dignified in his charcoal suit, scarcely glanced at the paper before saying "no" straight out.

Jane Thomson, an elderly member of the Fair Knitting Ladies group Carol belonged to with Laura, nodded in recognition at the picture. "I saw her at church on Sunday."

"Not since then?" Annemarie asked, crestfallen. After Jane shook her head, the girl shifted her focus to Jane's husband, Alastair. "Have you seen her, Mr. Thomson?"

"I saw her at the gas station yesterday," he said. "Hard to miss that green Saab of hers."

A nearby table full of senior ladies made similar comments. Molly had agreed to roll with Laura's idea of having a daily special, and that day's selection—white-haired customers could buy six Scottish snowballs, get one free—had been drawing in the elderly crowd all day.

Henry Roberts, also in a business suit despite the skyrocketing temperatures outside, folded the newspaper he'd been reading at a nearby table. He stood, then peered at the paper over the women's heads. "She reminds me of a customer I served in my store last week. Does she have a dog?"

"Yes!" Annemarie's demeanor brightened. "A springer spaniel."

Carol's attention jerked from the Abernethy biscuits she was boxing for her next customer back to Bridget's friend. Could she be looking for Jeanette?

"She takes the dog everywhere she goes," Annemarie went on. "Have you seen her today?"

Henry shook his head. "Sorry, can't say I have. My shop's closed on Wednesdays."

The young woman visibly deflated and returned to Bridget. "You've got to ask your bosses to help me find her."

Bridget cast a helpless glance at Carol.

"You said they're really good at solving mysteries," Annemarie pressed. "And they know my mom. She comes in here every week."

Carol gave her last customer his order and bustled over to the dining area. She introduced herself to Bridget's friend and asked if she might look at the picture.

When Annemarie handed it over, Carol's heart jolted in recognition. "Jeanette is your mom?"

"Yes," Annemarie said, her voice breaking. "Will you please help me find her?" The girl's eyes shone with fear and helplessness. "I'm afraid something terrible has happened."

2

Now that Carol stood face-to-face with Annemarie, she understood why the young woman had looked so familiar. She had her mother's nose and the same close-set eyes. But Jeanette's eyes had never looked quite so desperate.

"When did you last see your mother?" Carol asked gently.

"I talked to her on the phone last night," Annemarie said. "My neighbor told me she left the house this morning to take Scout for a hike."

"So she's been missing for six or seven hours?" Carol clarified. No wonder the police weren't concerned—but Annemarie clearly was.

Annemarie nodded miserably. "No one has seen her since early this morning, and she's not answering her phone. And she *always* has it with her."

"Cell reception can be spotty out on those hiking trails," Bridget said. "And on the lake. Maybe she went out on your boat?"

"No, I already checked." Impatience had crept into Annemarie's tone. "The boat is at its dock in the marina. I'm sure something must've happened to her."

"Is Scout missing too?" Carol asked.

"Yes," Annemarie said. "They were last seen together. And no one I've asked—and I've asked everyone I could find within ten miles of town—has seen a stray dog either."

Carol sucked in a deep breath, not sure how she and her partners could help Annemarie. Sure, they'd solved a mystery or two since moving to Loch Mallaig, but it wasn't like they were expert detectives or anything. This was a job for the police. Too bad they weren't willing to help.

"Perhaps your mom drove farther afield than usual," Carol suggested. "Maybe she forgot to charge her phone. Scout is such an energetic fellow. They could've gone on an extra-long excursion."

"Did she know you were coming home?" Bridget chimed in.

Seemingly on reflex, Annemarie crumpled her mom's photo in her fist. "No, I wanted to surprise her. I wasn't supposed to be home from summer session until Friday."

"So she wouldn't expect anyone to be worrying about her until your dad got home for supper," Carol said, feeling relieved that the situation didn't appear as ominous as Annemarie had made it sound.

"Mom and Dad are separated," Annemarie said dully.

Carol cringed at having reminded Annemarie of a clearly touchy subject. But it meant Jeanette had no reason to be home and no one to answer to concerning her whereabouts. "It's sounding more and more like you just need to wait her out."

"You don't understand!" the girl wailed.

Torn between helping the distressed girl and not letting her disturb the bakehouse's remaining customers, Carol glanced at the wall clock. It was closing time on the dot, and the few guests lingering at the sturdy Northwoods-style tables got up and left.

Carol guided Annemarie toward a clean table in the corner and urged her to sit. "How about you explain everything to me."

Bridget went to lock the front door, but stopped short at the window. "Um, Carol . . ."

Carol angled to peer out the window. Her eyes went wide when she saw a stream of hungry-looking tourists bouncing off a bus with *Yooper Express Tours* emblazoned on the side. Closing time was a relative concept in the face of all that revenue.

The front door opened, sunlight bouncing off its colorful stained glass design, and people flooded in. They made a beeline toward Molly at the counter, calling out orders in a sudden onslaught of chaos.

Carol squeezed Annemarie's hand. "I'm going to need you to wait a few more minutes while we take care of these customers. Bridget can bring you a nice cup of tea." While Bridget nodded and scurried off, Carol squeezed Annemarie's hand one more time then stood. "I'll return as soon as I can."

Just then, Hamish pulled up out front in the 1939 LaSalle hearse the bakehouse had repurposed as a delivery vehicle, and the tourists' chatter escalated. Tall and thin, or a *skinny malinky* as Carol's Scottish grandmother would've described him, Hamish stalked through the front door, his white hair clinging in a ring around his head from where his hat had sat. He'd been delivering bread to their restaurant customers, and without air-conditioning, it had likely been a steamy drive.

Hamish looked over the customers' heads until his blue-eyed gaze locked with Carol's. "Ack, could the *blethering* get any louder?" he exclaimed. He was born and raised in Loch Mallaig, but he spoke with a hint of a Scottish accent inherited from his parents that got more pronounced the more agitated he was.

An elderly tourist with flaming red hair beamed at Hamish. "You're Scottish too?" He tipped the last of his Empire biscuit into his mouth with a moan of pleasure. "This is *well tidy scran*, isn't it?"

Hamish nodded. "Aye, that it is."

"Delicious food," Carol translated to a bewildered-looking customer clearly unfamiliar with Scottishisms, then she signaled to Hamish. "Could you please clear the rest of the tables? We don't have room for all these customers to eat in, but we should do our best."

Hamish went straight to work bussing tables. He could be surly, but he was a hard worker with a soft side.

"I'll help fill orders as soon as I give this tea to Annemarie," Bridget told Carol as she passed her, teacup in hand.

"That's okay," Carol said. "If she needs you, we can manage."

Carol joined Laura and Molly behind the counter and rang up the orders while her friends boxed them. Fortunately, the bus driver had only given his passengers a fifteen-minute window, so the group took all their orders to go, easing Hamish's load considerably.

Angus, who seemed to sense when the clock struck three, had snuck downstairs, and he delighted in discreetly trailing Hamish as he bussed the tables.

"Is that upstairs doorjamb swollen from the humidity again?" Hamish groused. "The door's always popping open and out you come to pester me, laddie." He sounded gruff, but a moment later he slipped the Scottie a bit of piecrust left behind on one of the plates. Was it any wonder the dog adored him?

A few minutes later, they ushered their last customer out the door and locked it behind him.

Laura whistled as she came around the counter and assessed the display cases. "That group cleared out almost all our stock."

"Tourist season is in full swing," Molly said as she closed out the till.

Apparently done calculating what she'd need to do to restock the cases for the next day, Laura glanced up. Her gaze rested on Annemarie, then she raised an eyebrow at Carol. "Did the bus forget somebody?"

"No," Carol began. "That's—"

"I need your help," Annemarie broke in, springing to her feet. "My mom left this morning to take her dog for a walk, and no one has seen or heard from her since. I've driven all around the county looking for her car at the usual spots she likes to hike, and I showed her picture around town." Annemarie's explanation spilled out, the words toppling over each other in her breathless attempt to not miss a single detail.

Angus planted himself next to Annemarie, leaning into her leg. He licked her hand as if to offer comfort. Or maybe he knew his pal Scout was missing along with Jeanette and he was commiserating.

"The police said they couldn't help you?" Laura clarified.

"They said a competent adult has to be gone for forty-eight hours before they're considered missing unless there is evidence of foul play." Tears dribbled down Annemarie's cheeks, and Bridget handed her a paper napkin from a nearby dispenser.

Molly frowned. "I see."

"No you don't," Annemarie argued. "Foul play is exactly what I'm afraid has happened."

Foul play? Carol had listened to Annemarie's fractured explanation of her mother's disappearance twice now, and nothing in it suggested foul play. An accident while hiking in the woods perhaps, but is that what Annemarie meant?

Hamish flipped the sign in the window to *Closed* and cleared his throat. "Seems to me we should all sit down and let Miss Franklin explain exactly what happened leading up to her mother's disappearance."

"Thanks, Mr. Bruce," Annemarie said gratefully.

"You were a conscientious student, Annemarie," Hamish said, apparently having taught her when he was still working at the local high school. "Unless you've gone daft since high school, I assume your concerns aren't baseless."

Molly poured six glasses of water and filled a plate with the remaining cookies from the display case. She carried them over to the table where Annemarie sat with Bridget.

Once they'd all taken a seat, Hamish nodded at Annemarie. "Okay, now start at the beginning."

Annemarie drew in a deep breath and flattened the picture of her mom in the middle of the table. "My mom is Jeanette Franklin."

Annemarie recapped what she'd told Carol and Bridget earlier. "Since Mom wasn't expecting me home until Friday, I didn't start to worry about her until she didn't return for lunch and I couldn't reach her on the phone. I always call her at lunch, and she never misses my call." She looked from one person to the next around the table. "Never."

Carol's chest grew heavy. Annemarie hadn't mentioned that part earlier.

"After both texting and phoning for half an hour with no response, I called my dad," Annemarie went on. "He said Mom probably went shopping. But she had Scout with her, and it's superhot outside, so she'd never leave him tied outside the shops in the middle of the day, let alone in a hot car. He said she probably went to her sister's then, or to a friend's. So I tried calling Aunt Karen and Mom's friends. None of her friends had seen her and there was no answer at my aunt's."

"Could she have left Scout at your aunt's while they went shopping?" Bridget asked.

"It's possible. But she wouldn't ignore her phone. And I've been trying it all afternoon. By now she would've realized she missed my lunchtime call and checked for messages, charged her phone if that had been the problem."

"She didn't mention to your father what her plans for the day were?" Molly asked.

"They're separated," Carol whispered.

"Oh I'm sorry." Molly exchanged a glance with Carol, no doubt wondering the same thing as she was—did Annemarie suspect her father of the foul play she'd mentioned?

"I've spent every minute since searching the countryside for Mom's old green Saab. It's pretty memorable, but no one has seen it anywhere."

"Isn't this the day Jeanette usually comes in for her oatcakes?" Hamish asked.

Carol shook her head. "That's tomorrow. Thursdays."

"That's when she gets her alimony check from Dad." Annemarie glowered. "I mean, 'separate maintenance.' That's what they call it for couples who aren't divorced yet."

Carol gritted her teeth, not liking how convenient it was Jeanette should go missing the day before the next check was due.

Molly, who had a twentysomething daughter of her own, turned sympathetic eyes on Annemarie, but didn't speak. Perhaps she had no idea what to say.

Carol was at a loss too. Annemarie still hadn't divulged what she thought might be the nature of the foul play she was certain had befallen her mother. "Annemarie, you mentioned foul play. Are you thinking of something specific?"

Annemarie cringed. "It could be anything, couldn't it? That's what I need you to figure out. Mom adopted Scout soon after she and Dad separated. She already hated being alone in the house when I was away at school, and she was worried that living alone made her a target. What if someone was stalking her or something?"

"You think she was being watched?" Hamish tapped his fingers on the table, his lips pinching as if he'd swallowed something sour. "Sometimes spouses hire private investigators to spy on each other for evidence to use in divorce court. Do you think that's something your dad might've done?"

Annemarie shook her head. "Dad didn't want the separation. It was Mom's idea."

"It's hot out," Molly said. "Jeanette could've gone to the beach. I always leave my phone in the car when I go to the beach because I don't want to drop it in the water. She could've just lost track of time."

"Annemarie searched the parking lots for her mom's car at all the local beaches," Bridget reminded them.

"Okay," Carol said, wanting to make sure she had all the facts straight about Annemarie's request for help. "So you want us to find evidence your mom is a victim of foul play?"

Annemarie nodded.

"But there is no evidence of a struggle at the house?" Carol asked. "No reports of your mother's car being found abandoned somewhere?"

"Not that I know of."

Carol's mind cataloged all the tidbits. "Based on that, let's assume it's more likely that she went hiking somewhere, was injured somehow, and can't call for help because she's out of cell phone range."

Although Hamish merely sat with one hand scratching his neat, white goatee, apparently lost in thought, Molly and Laura nodded in agreement.

"That's what I first thought." Annemarie trembled. "But then I should've found her car at one of the trailheads."

"Unless she went to a place you didn't think to check," Carol said, aware that even longtime residents didn't always seem to appreciate the enormity of the forested areas in the Upper Peninsula.

Annemarie bit her lip. "I can't stand the thought that she's out in the woods in pain with no way to get help. Surely by now Scout would've attracted attention to her with his barking. She doesn't go on remote trails."

Carol glanced out the window. The blistering heat had zapped the energy from the now-limp petunias in the flower baskets on the lampposts. It wasn't the kind of day many people would opt for a strenuous hike over relaxing on the water.

"I—we—know an avid outdoorsman who's lived here all his life," Molly said, no doubt referring to Fergus MacGregor, the handsome owner of the Castleglen golf resort and lodge. "I could ask him if there are lesser known trails he'd suggest we check."

"I have a few ideas myself," Hamish added gruffly, reminding them tacitly that he'd lived in the area a whole lot longer than any of them. Carol imagined his love of bird-watching had taken him on many a hike over the years. "I'll drive around to a few and check for your mother's car."

Still clutching her napkin, Annemarie dabbed at her damp eyes. "Thank you. I can't stand sitting around doing nothing when I know she must be out there somewhere, probably hurt. I did check with the hospital, but she hasn't been admitted. And the police said there'd been no traffic accidents in the county today, so that's reassuring at least."

"You should drop by your dad's office, lass," Hamish said. "He might be able to suggest other places your mom would go."

"I'll come with you," Bridget volunteered.

Annemarie pulled her keys from her purse and handed them to Bridget. "Do you mind driving? I'm a mess."

After the pair left, Carol glanced at each of her friends. "What do you think?"

"I hope Jeanette went out of town with a friend and isn't lying hurt in the woods somewhere," Molly said.

"Me too," Laura agreed. "I don't see why the police wouldn't at least be willing to issue a BOLO for her car."

"Maybe because she's a grown woman." Hamish pushed his chair back and stood. "A grown woman who might not want to be found at the moment. I'll still go drive past my favorite obscure haunts and see if I can find her, though."

"Thanks, Hamish." Carol motioned to the tables he'd cleared and wiped spotless. Whether it was renovations, repairs, or run-of-the-mill chores, he did all his tasks at the bakery meticulously. "For everything."

His lips curled at the corners as he slapped on his tartan cap, betraying a crack in the curmudgeonly veneer he seemed so fond of projecting.

Already feeling too tired for the work yet to be finished before they could leave, Carol forced herself up from her chair. "Those dishes aren't going to wash themselves."

Molly collected the tray of untouched water glasses from the center of the table. "I wonder if the cell phone company could ping Jeanette's phone to locate her."

Laura trailed them into the kitchen. "They wouldn't do it without a warrant. Or do you have a connection in the phone company we don't know about?" she teased.

Molly shook her head. "Sadly, no."

An idea came to Carol, but she bristled at the implications. Still, it might be worth pursuing. "I don't like to think it, but I can't help wondering if there's a clue to a secret liaison in Jeanette's computer or journal. A liaison she wouldn't want Annemarie to know about."

"So you think Hamish is right?" Laura asked.

Carol shrugged. "As much as I don't want it to be the case, is it worse than her lying injured in a forest somewhere unable to move or call for help?"

Just as the last of the dishes had been put away, Carol's cell phone rang. She glanced at the screen and her hope surged. "It's Bridget." She connected the call and immediately asked, "Good news?"

"Sorry but no," Bridget answered, tentacles of tension in her voice. "I actually have a bad feeling."

"What happened?"

"Mr. Franklin was abrupt and impatient with Annemarie when we showed up at his office. He was really dismissive, telling her he was in the middle of an important business meeting even though she was obviously upset."

Carol's heart squeezed for the poor girl. "Some men can't stand tears."

"She's his daughter!" Bridget snapped. Her voice softened almost immediately. "I'm sorry."

"I don't blame you. It's a stressful situation and it doesn't help that he doesn't seem to be taking it seriously," Carol said gently.

"Yeah," Bridget replied. "I was just thinking. There was something *off* about the way her dad acted."

"Off how?"

"I can't explain it. It's just a feeling I have." Bridget released an audibly troubled exhale. "I think he knows more about Jeanette's disappearance than he's letting on."

3

Carol made a quick decision. "I was just about to leave the bakery. I'll swing by Annemarie's house and help you look for any clues Jeanette might have left about where she went."

"Would you?" Bridget quickly recited the address, as if fearful Carol might change her mind.

"I'll see you soon," Carol promised. She asked Molly and Laura if they wanted to come along, but they both declined, telling her to go ahead without them since time was of the essence. Laura had a lot of work to do in the kitchen after the tourists had bought them out, and Molly had to finalize a new brochure and send the file to the printer.

Carol grabbed her purse from the kitchen, then went out the back door to her car. She quickly sent her husband, Harvey, a text letting him know she wouldn't be home at her usual time, then set out for the Franklins' house.

Ten minutes later, Carol had followed her GPS navigation's cues along Yooper Boulevard, which curved around Loch Mallaig's namesake lake, and down a side street to a long, winding driveway. She steered onto it, then gasped when an enormous, two-story stone home appeared. She'd had no idea how wealthy Jeanette was. Evidently Mr. Franklin's business was quite successful—and that in itself could be stressful, so it explained why he'd be terse with Annemarie if she was interrupting an important meeting.

Carol frowned as she parked her Chrysler 300 and stared at the massive house. What if someone had planned to kidnap Jeanette for ransom or burglarize the house and something had gone wrong?

Bridget appeared at the oversize oak front door and beckoned Carol inside.

Carol shut off the engine, climbed out of the car, and hurried up the porch steps. "Did you find any clues?"

"Not yet." Bridget stepped back to let Carol in to the expansive foyer, which had a wide staircase and opened into a great room, dining room, and kitchen. At first glance, everything appeared to be in order. "Annemarie is calling Scout's vet now to find out if the dog had a checkup scheduled for today."

"He didn't." Annemarie emerged from the kitchen, shoulders slumped and eyes still red.

"Let's have a look around," Carol said in her most encouraging voice. She slipped off her shoes so she wouldn't soil the plush cream-colored carpet in the airy great room overlooking Loch Mallaig. "Wow, what an incredible view." The rippling water was inky even though the sun was hours from dipping below the pine spires on the distant shore.

Annemarie peered out the floor-to-ceiling windows, but the dullness never left her eyes. "Mom and Dad used to sit on the dock at night and watch the sunset together when we first moved here," she murmured. "It seems like ages ago."

The house phone rang and Annemarie appeared immediately hopeful. She dashed toward the kitchen.

"Let's hope that's her mom," Carol said.

"You can say that again." With crossed arms, Bridget rubbed her bare biceps as if she couldn't get warm.

While they waited for Annemarie, Carol slowly pivoted where she stood, taking in the rest of the room, which included a walnut coffee table with dovetail construction and obviously hand-carved details.

"Oh, look at that table. It's gorgeous."

"That's what I said when I saw it too," Bridget said. "It's so unique."

"I wonder if it's the table Jeanette bought from the new antiques shop."

"It is," Annemarie said, returning to the room.

"We should see if we can find something like that for the bakery," Bridget said.

"Molly wants to stop by the shop," Carol said, "but I'm reluctant to rouse Doreen's annoyance when she's feeling the pinch of the antiques shop's popularity, especially with a piece everyone would notice and ask about."

Bridget shrugged, then turned her attention to Annemarie. "Who was on the phone?"

"My mom's friend Melody," Annemarie said. "I left her a voice mail earlier asking if she'd seen Mom today, but she hasn't. And she had no suggestions where she might've gone with Scout besides the places I already checked."

Carol squared her shoulders. "Then let's go through the house and see if we can find a clue to where else she might've gone. Where does your mom keep her appointment book?"

"In the kitchen." Annemarie led the way into a massive kitchen with an extra-wide gas stove, granite countertops, and perfectly polished copper pots hanging over the center island. Annemarie opened a drawer near the phone. "This is Mom's catchall drawer."

In addition to a leather-bound personal organizer, she pulled out miscellaneous slips of paper, multiple address books, outdated calendars, and instruction manuals and piled them on the counter.

Carol leafed through the appointment book first. The month of July was blank except for a handful of birthday reminders. "It's Melody Carver's birthday today. Is she the woman you just talked to?"

"Yes." Annemarie's forehead furrowed. "It's not like Mom to forget a birthday. She always drops by with flowers or chocolates to celebrate."

"Hey, check this out." Bridget had picked up a leaflet advertising a stage play in a nearby town. "Today's date is circled. Maybe your mom went to the lunchtime matinee."

Carol skimmed the information. "It would explain why her phone's not on. They always ask you to turn them off before a performance. Maybe she forgot to power it back up."

"But then where is Scout?" Annemarie countered. "He wouldn't be allowed in the theater. And Aunt Karen doesn't like to have animals in the house at the best of times, so I can't imagine Mom leaving him at her house on his own."

"Perhaps they planned to make a full day of it," Carol suggested. "Maybe they were going to shop and get dinner with your mom spending the night afterward, in which case she wouldn't want to leave Scout here alone that whole time."

Annemarie shook her head. "Her overnight bag is still in the closet." She motioned to the dog bowls by the door. "She didn't pack Scout's dishes either. And her toothbrush and insulin are still in the bathroom. She's got diabetes." Annemarie's bottom lip trembled. "It's almost suppertime. She could get seriously ill without her medicine."

"Could she have just taken a couple of doses along?" Carol asked.

"Maybe," Annemarie admitted. "She did tell me she just got a to-go kit so she could take it hiking with her. But I don't think it held very much."

Carol pressed her lips together, more concerned that Jeanette's blood sugar might dip too low if she were lying injured out in the woods, unable to eat. But it wasn't a scenario Annemarie needed to hear.

She glanced at her watch. "It's still early. When my chickens escape their pen, I may not see hide nor feather of them all day, but come dusk, they always mosey back to their coop." She and Harvey had decided to try raising chickens when they moved to Loch Mallaig, and the three birds frequently gave them trouble of one kind or another.

"Hey, there's an answering machine over here," Bridget called from the adjacent laundry room. Apparently she'd slipped away to do some more investigating. "And the light is flashing."

"I forgot about that," Annemarie said as she and Carol joined Bridget. "Mom set it up to screen her calls after Dad moved out. He doesn't have her new cell number, so he always calls this one." Annemarie pressed the button.

"Jeanie, if you'd let me come home, you wouldn't have to worry about alimony checks," Mr. Franklin's terse voice boomed over the line. "I always gave you all the spending money you wanted, didn't I? I will bring the check around Thursday as usual. Just use a credit card in the meantime if you have to."

Carol cringed at the impatience in his tone. *But he wants to come home.* That didn't sound like a man who'd make his wife disappear. Unless he was the kind of man who expected things his way or else. Carol's own husband was an easygoing retired journalist who now contentedly sold handmade fishing lures online, but she knew not all men were as even-keeled as Harvey.

Carol bit her bottom lip, hesitant to ask the question gnawing at her thoughts.

With no such qualms, Bridget blurted, "Has your dad ever hurt your mom?"

Annemarie stiffened. "No way! Dad only hurt her by caring more about his company than her." She gestured at the impressive kitchen. "Mom didn't ask for all of this. She would've been happier in a trailer if it meant Dad didn't leave the house before breakfast and stay at work until after bedtime. He bought a boat he never has time to sail and a big-screen TV he never takes time to watch. About the only thing he's bought that he actually uses is the personal gym downstairs, but he prefers to work out alone, before Mom and I are up. She said she was tired of competing with his business for his attention."

"I understand that," Carol murmured.

Bridget, however, wasn't appeased. "If he's worried about his image, maybe he's not happy with being made to look as if he can't hold his marriage together."

"Dad has his problems," Annemarie said. "I know that. But he'd never hurt Mom. He loves her. I think he's finally starting to realize how lost he is without her. How all the success in the world is meaningless if he doesn't have someone to share it with."

Bridget grimaced. "I don't like to speak ill of your father. I hope you know that. I just think if you're worried about foul play, we have to consider the possibility."

Carol expelled a breath. "Your father is the first person authorities would investigate in a situation like this."

Annemarie pulled her phone from her pocket. "I'm going to try my aunt again. I think you might be right about Mom going to see the play."

Bridget shot Carol a helpless glance.

Carol squeezed her shoulder encouragingly. "Have you walked through the whole house and the garage?"

Bridget nodded. "I can show you. Maybe you'll see something we overlooked."

But Carol didn't. When they joined Annemarie in the kitchen again, Carol said, "There's no sign of a struggle. Perhaps more importantly, there's no sign that an attempt has been made to cover one up by cleaning." Carol pointed to the floor. "The house basically looks as if it's due for its weekly cleaning. And the dirt and dust seems evenly distributed, not like one section of carpet or floor has been scrubbed to hide a scuffle."

Bridget peeked in the garbage pail. "There's no broken glass or anything dumped in here either. I do see coffee grounds and an empty milk carton, so it was last emptied before breakfast."

Annemarie gave up on her phone call with a sigh of frustration. "Still no answer."

"Is there anything that seems out of place or missing?" Carol asked Annemarie.

"You mean like if it were knocked over and the intruder didn't know where to put it back?" Annemarie asked, apparently better able to cope with the possibility of an intruder striking her mother and trying to cover it up than her father. She glanced around the kitchen, then walked from room to room on the first floor, once more surveying each with a critical eye. As she completed her examination of the great room, she frowned. "No. Everything seems to be in its place."

"Does your mother have a computer?" Carol asked.

Annemarie nodded. "And I even know the password." She pulled the laptop from a nearby shelf, set it on the coffee table, and booted it up. "She didn't e-mail much, but she liked to browse gardening sites."

"I noticed the lovely flower bed along the front of the house," Carol said. "She has quite a variety of unique flowers."

"Almost all of them are somehow medicinal," Annemarie explained, sounding proud of her mother's hobby. "She dries the flowers, leaves, or roots—whatever has healing properties—to make various teas and tinctures."

"They really work too," Bridget interjected. "I started coming down with that horrible flu that was going around just before midterms, and Annemarie gave me a bottle of her mom's elderberry syrup. I was as good as new in no time."

"I'll have to try that next time I feel something coming on," Carol said. "I hate that feeling of knowing you're starting to get sick and not being able to do a thing to stop it from happening."

On the verge of tears once more, Annemarie appeared as if she felt the same way about her mother's current situation.

"Let's take a look at your mom's e-mails first, shall we?" Carol suggested. "If that doesn't turn up any clues, then we can explore Jeanette's browsing history."

The three ladies clustered around the laptop while Annemarie typed in the password. A few clicks later, Jeanette's e-mail program came up on screen.

Bridget's eyes widened the instant Jeanette's inbox populated itself with messages. "Your mom has e-mails from Puppy Love. That's a dating site for dog lovers."

"No way," Annemarie said emphatically.

Bridget pointed to the subject heading of an e-mail from earlier in the week. *[PL] Evening dog date soon?* She pointed to the acronym in brackets. "This is how messages come in from the dating site. Would-be suitors send messages to the profile's mailbox, and the dating site forwards them to your personal e-mail. It offers a barrier of protection from creeps."

Annemarie clicked open the message and skimmed it. "This sounds as if they've already corresponded a couple of times before. He says he takes his sheltie to the leash-free dog park in Loch Mallaig every evening between six and seven, and maybe she could stop by sometime and join him."

"That came in Monday night," Bridget said. "So perhaps she went to the park last night and met him. If they hit it off, they might've made plans to spend today together." Bridget winced at her friend's pained expression. She added in an apologetic tone, "It would explain why she's ignoring her phone."

"Or," Annemarie said, wheels turning, "what if that's true, but Mom decided the guy was a creep? Or realized she couldn't date another guy when she was still technically married to Dad? Maybe the guy couldn't handle her rejection. He could've followed her home and stalked her this morning as she left the house. He could've shadowed her on her morning walk, maybe staying back or keeping it real casual until they were deep in the woods, well away from any other hikers."

"Annemarie, don't," Carol cautioned, not wanting the girl to get caught up in painful conjecture. "Don't do that to yourself."

"Why not?" Annemarie frowned. "Isn't that how sleuths solve problems? You imagine possibilities and then either prove them true or rule them out. It could happen." She shivered, then hugged herself and stared out at the dark lake. Storm clouds gathered above the water, mirrored in the glossy surface. "You hear about stuff like that in the news," she went on, her voice now scarcely above a shaky whisper. "And if Mom rebuffed him again, who knows what he might've done?"

Carol wavered over their next move. It was barely five o'clock, so finding Jeanette's Puppy Love pen pal at the dog park with his sheltie between six and seven was a logical next step. But given Annemarie's wild imagination, she wasn't sure bringing her along would be a good idea.

Bridget put an arm around her friend's shoulder. "I hate to think of you here alone. Do you want to spend the night at my house?" she asked. "We can check in with Hamish and Molly after supper to find out if they came up with any other hiking areas we should check out, or we could post missing flyers around town."

"I think I should stay here, in case Mom comes home or calls." Annemarie glanced at her cell phone screen for the umpteenth time.

"Why don't you bunk here?" Carol suggested to Bridget, praying her own initial speculation about Jeanette's attacker burglarizing the place was totally off base. She made a mental note to call the police and suggest they send extra patrols through the area.

"I'm good with that. Is that okay with you?" Bridget asked Annemarie.

"That would be nice." Annemarie offered a wan smile of gratitude. "I can drive you home to pick up your things and we could grab takeout for supper."

"Print some more photos and take them with you," Carol urged. "It never hurts to ask people if they've seen your mom. I'll visit the dog park and see if the sheltie owner turns up."

Annemarie's brisk inhale put Carol on edge. "We should come with you."

"I think if he knows something, he's more likely to let it slip out if he doesn't feel as if it's an inquisition," Carol reasoned.

Annemarie deflated. "I guess you're right."

"Don't worry. I'll let you know what I learn, if anything," Carol said. "And be careful here. Be sure you keep all the doors and windows locked and the alarm set." She hesitated, not wanting to unduly worry them but knowing they needed to be on their guard. "If someone did hurt your mom, they might assume the house is empty and would be easy to loot," she added softly.

Bridget shuddered. "Are you sure you wouldn't rather stay at my house, Annemarie?"

Annemarie almost chuckled. "We'll be okay. Dad's alarm system will scare off the most brazen burglar. Mom never sets it, but I know how to."

Carol gave Bridget an encouraging sideways hug. "Just stick together and you'll be fine."

After texting Molly about meeting at the dog park, Carol hurried home, checking the clock and trying to think of a supper she could make quickly for her and Harvey before she left again. *I could defrost that leftover Scotch broth from last month,* she thought, then wrinkled her nose when she saw the car's temperature gauge was reading in the high 80s. Not exactly soup weather.

As she pulled into the driveway of their log home, Harvey came out of the house wearing a khaki fishing vest and a smile for his wife. He waved, then snatched up his fishing rod and tackle box from the front porch. He met her in the driveway with a warm embrace. "What a lucky surprise," he said. "Based on your text, I wasn't expecting you home until later."

"I thought I'd pop by and make dinner before my next stop," Carol told him.

"Too late. I already made myself a sandwich with that leftover roasted chicken. Made you one too while I had everything out."

"Thank you, honey." Carol patted his cheek. "I knew I kept you around for a reason."

"Speaking of being around, I was headed out fishing, but I can come with you on your errand if you want. So one of your customers went missing?"

Carol nodded. "It's one of our regulars, Jeanette Franklin. Her daughter, Annemarie, is a friend of Bridget's, and the poor girl is worried sick." Carol explained the situation in more detail. "I thought Molly and I might take Angus to the dog park and see what we can learn from the man with the sheltie."

Harvey's eyes narrowed. "Are you sure that's safe?"

"Angus will protect us."

Harvey laughed heartily. He and Angus were good buddies, and it was unlikely Harvey could picture the wee Scottie doing anything but cuddling a threatening person into submission.

"Enjoy your fishing." Carol gave him another hug. "And don't worry about me."

Harvey shook his head. "That's like asking me not to breathe."

Carol hurried inside to change into jeans. She grabbed a lightweight jacket in case the evening gave them a reprieve from the heat, then bustled toward the bedroom door.

As she passed, a paw reached out from under the bed and swatted at her foot.

She squealed in surprise. "Pascal, I wish you would stop doing that." She bent down to peek under the dust ruffle. Although Pascal often felt comfortable cuddling up to Carol as she slept, the occasional swat at a passerby was as brave as the shy gray-and-white cat got during waking hours. "You hungry?"

His meow sounded indifferent.

"Suit yourself." She straightened. "I'll put out a fresh bowl. Come help yourself when you're ready." Carol went to the kitchen and tipped fresh kibbles into Pascal's bowl, then poured herself a glass of water and grabbed the plate Harvey had left in the refrigerator for her. *Such a thoughtful man.*

Carol texted with Molly as she ate the sandwich, and they agreed to meet at Bread on Arrival in fifteen minutes. When she was done, she put the plate in the dishwasher. "I'm going out," she called to Pascal, although he seemed to care as little about her comings and goings as he did about dinner.

On the way to the bakehouse, Molly called the police station and asked if they would patrol Annemarie's street. Wilma Guthrie, the chatty receptionist who traced her ancestry to Alexander Graham Bell, peppered Carol with questions about Jeanette's disappearance. She remained noncommittal about the extra patrols but promised to pass along the request to the officers on duty.

Ten minutes later, Carol climbed the bakery's exterior stairs that led to Molly's second-story apartment and knocked on the door.

The sound of little paws scampering across the floor filtered through the door, then Molly appeared a moment later. "Hold your horses," she told Angus, scooping him up before he could run out. She snapped on a leash, then set him back down and raised an eyebrow at Carol. "Now what's this all about?"

As Carol drove them to the dog park, she explained about the man with the sheltie who'd been corresponding with Jeanette and his nightly routine.

"So you want to question him?" Molly asked.

"Yes. And if he seems shady, maybe ask others there what they know about him."

Molly shivered. "Do we really want to introduce ourselves to a man who could be a kidnapper . . . or worse?"

Carol shrugged. "I'd like to think he's just one of those suspects that need to be eliminated if we're going to be thorough."

"If there are any 'suspects' at all." Molly sighed. "I feel bad that Annemarie is so worried, and I hope it's over nothing. The most likely scenario is still that Jeanette is probably far afield, enjoying the day, believing she has no one to answer to."

"Did Fergus get back to you with any ideas for hiking trails she might have gone on?"

"He gave me a huge list, but when I passed it along, Annemarie said she'd already checked the parking areas for every last one of them. That makes me think she just drove farther away from town than usual."

"I hope you're right," Carol said. "Fingers crossed that soon Jeanette will see her phone messages and check in with Annemarie to set the poor girl's wild imagination at ease."

Molly scratched Angus's scruffy neck. "But we're still going to chat with Mr. Sheltie Owner."

"His name is Steve."

"Sounds innocuous enough." Molly stuck out her bottom lip and blew her long blonde bangs from her eyes. "I can't think of any infamous hardened criminals who go by Steve."

Carol chuckled. "We'll be fine."

"We'd better be," Molly said with mock sternness. "My brother is expecting to see me in Iowa next week. Chloe is even driving in from Milwaukee to join us for the weekend and see her cousins."

"And her mother." Carol was so grateful her own daughter lived in Loch Mallaig with her family. Before Carol retired from her job in

Pittsburgh, she'd hated being so far away from her grandchildren, and now she saw them at least a few times a week.

"I'm glad she can take time off. It can be hard with a new job, but Chloe says her boss at the veterinary practice is very pleased with how she's doing." Molly's voice adopted a slightly faraway quality. "Kevin would've been so proud of her." More than a decade had passed since Molly's husband's untimely death, enabling Molly to talk about him fondly without the melancholy that had marked the first few difficult years when Chloe was a teenager.

"Mom's proud too." Carol glanced over and grinned.

Molly smiled back. "Of course."

The dog park came into view just beyond the high school, and Carol slowed her car. "Lots of people here. I think I'll park on the road." She pulled over just before the entrance to the lot.

Molly climbed out with Angus tucked under her arm. "No old green Saab in the lot."

"That would've been too easy," Carol said. "I do see a sheltie romping around in the field though. With any luck, that pup belongs to Steve."

Molly set Angus down once they reached the parking area and he raced ahead, tugging at his leash. "I see someone's ready to join the party."

Carol chuckled. "Whisper in his ear that we need him to make friends with a certain sheltie."

"Sure, why not?" Molly stepped into the fenced play area and Carol closed the gate behind them. As Molly leaned down to unhook Angus's leash, she pointed to the Shetland sheepdog with a long nose and silky white and brown fur. "That looks like a nice little friend for you to introduce yourself to."

As if he understood, Angus frolicked toward the sheltie and they greeted each other with a bout of enthusiastic sniffing before racing off together.

While Carol lingered near the fence, Molly walked over to the middle-aged man who seemed to be keeping an eye on the sheltie. "Is the sheltie yours?" she asked.

He nodded. "That's Jinx. The Scottie is yours?"

"Yep, Angus. He loves making new friends."

They stood in amiable silence, watching the dogs. Instead of joining them, Carol stood back so she could study the man's reactions to Molly's questions . . . if she ever got around to asking any.

After a few moments, Molly ventured, "You wouldn't happen to be the sheltie owner my friend Jeanette told me about meeting online, would you?"

The man had sandy blond hair and at least half a foot on Molly's petite frame. He cocked his head and looked down at her. "That's right. I'm Steve."

"I'm Molly. I heard Jeanette planned to meet you here yesterday. How'd it go?"

"She did?" A smile left a dimple in Steve's cheek. "She never showed. But I'm happy to hear she'd planned to."

"I hope she didn't get cold feet."

He glanced toward the gate. "Maybe she'll come tonight. But no springer spaniels so far."

"I think she must've gone out of town," Molly said. "I haven't seen her or heard from her all day."

Steve seemed to deflate. "There's always tomorrow, I guess."

"I certainly hope so," Molly said, and Carol felt the gravity of the words.

Angus chose that moment to race after another dog toward the other end of the park, giving Molly a natural reason to excuse herself.

"I'd better go keep an eye on him," she told Steve, then crossed the grass.

Carol strolled along the fence line to catch up to Molly. "So what do you think?" she asked quietly.

Molly glanced back toward Steve. "I don't think he's ever met Jeanette. If I'm wrong and he's kidnapped her or something, he's the coolest customer I've ever seen."

"I got the same impression—that he's simply eager to meet her. He was clearly disappointed when you said she was out of town today."

"Now what?" Molly asked.

Carol reached into her pocket and removed the photo of Jeanette that Annemarie had given her. "We could show Jeanette's picture to the other dog owners, ask if anyone has seen her or her car or her dog today."

"I'd better not do that or Steve will put two and two together," Molly said. "And maybe don't mention Jeanette's name either. Just show people the picture."

Carol circulated among the pet owners. A few recognized Jeanette from around town and knew Scout, but they all said they'd never seen her at the leash-free park. When she'd discreetly chatted with everyone, Carol went to the gate, where Molly was clipping a leash onto Angus's collar while he sat leaning against her shin.

"Looks like you had fun," Carol said to Angus, who panted happily in response.

"Too much, I think." Molly scratched him behind his ears, then stood. "But he'll sleep well tonight."

As they walked to the car, Carol folded her photo of Jeanette and put it back in her pocket. "It doesn't sound as if Jeanette's ever been here."

"I guess we can safely cross Steve off the suspect list then," Molly said. "He wouldn't have been able to stalk her if he'd never seen her, right?"

Carol glanced back toward the park. "Just to be sure, maybe we could wait until he leaves and follow him home. What do you think?"

Molly scooped Angus into her arms with a grin. "That sounds like it could be interesting."

"Well, he seems like a nice guy . . . but that makes me wonder why he's still single."

"Hey." Molly scoffed playfully. "I'm a nice girl and I'm single. Laura too."

Carol rolled her eyes. "You know what I mean."

Molly continued to give her a hard time as they settled into the car and waited, watching the parking lot from their spot on the road.

Twenty minutes later, Steve opened the gate and exited the field with his sheltie.

"I bet he drives that electric-blue sports car," Molly said.

"He seems more like the black pickup type," Carol countered.

He proved them both wrong and deposited his small sheltie in the handlebar basket of an old-fashioned touring bike.

"I didn't see that one coming," Molly said.

Steve set out at a fast clip, the wind ruffling Jinx's fur.

"You'd better let him get well ahead," Molly said as Carol started the ignition. "If we trail him too closely, he'll see us."

They followed him down Loch Ness Lane, past the middle and elementary schools and closer to downtown. After about a mile, Steve parked his bike in front of a youth center and lifted Jinx out of her basket.

"Do you think he lives here?" Molly peered up at the tired-looking brick building. "He's not exactly a youth."

With Jinx beside him on a leash, Steve paused on the porch steps to chat briefly with a teen girl bouncing a basketball, then let himself inside.

"Let's go find out." With Molly and Angus close behind, Carol quickly caught up to the teen with the ball. "Excuse me. Do you know Steve?"

"Sure," the girl said. "Everyone knows Steve Gambel. He's one of our favorite volunteers."

"Do you know where he lives?" Molly asked.

"Cute dog." The teen squatted down and gave Angus a thorough petting, which he, of course, lapped up. "Why do you want to know about Steve?"

"Oh." Carol glanced at Molly, and it was clear they were both mentally clamoring for a legitimate excuse. "Someone ordered a box of cookies from our bakery for him to honor his volunteer work. Unfortunately, they didn't tell us where to deliver it."

"You could bring it here," the girl suggested.

"Yes," Molly interjected, "but we wouldn't want the other volunteers who don't get a gift to feel unappreciated because he was singled out."

"That makes sense." The teen gave Angus one last pat, then pushed to her feet. "He lives at the Pines and Needles trailer park. I don't know the number, but it's the red trailer with the red, white, and blue deck in front. If you take the cookies to the office, I'm sure they'll get to him."

"Thank you." Carol smiled. "You've been a tremendous help."

The teen started bouncing the ball again. "No problem."

Once they were back in the car, Carol sighed. "I wish we hadn't had to lie to the poor girl to get the information."

"It's for a good cause. We have Jeanette's welfare at heart, remember." Molly grinned. "And we could always send him cookies for real if you feel that bad about it."

They drove to the trailer park, which was about a half mile down Arran Road. Once inside the small, well-kept community, they had no trouble spotting the red trailer with the patriotic deck. Carol pulled into the guest parking lot, then she and Molly walked with Angus to Steve's trailer, where they regarded the deck—and furtively peeked in the windows for any evidence of Jeanette or Scout.

"It's pretty spartan inside," Molly said. "No sign of Jeanette."

Another passerby noticed them admiring the deck and paused. "It's eye-catching, isn't it?" The elderly man chuckled. "Steve is always coming up with unique ways to celebrate the Fourth of July. This one will last all year long."

"Very creative," Molly said. "Maybe next year he'll paint his car red, white, and blue."

"His bike maybe," the man corrected. "Steve doesn't have a car. Likes to live simply. You'd never know he owns one of the busiest heating and air-conditioning businesses in the Upper Peninsula."

"Really?" Carol's heart flinched a little at the news. For one, Annemarie's father owned the same kind of business, which was an odd coincidence to say the least. Not to mention that while Steve may not own a car, he'd certainly have access to his company's service vehicles.

"Yes, indeed," the man continued. "He donates most of his profits to the youth center and helps out there all he can too. He's a good man."

Molly scooped up Angus and tucked him under her arm. "We'd better be going."

Carol glanced around, trying to figure out the reason for Molly's sudden hurry.

"I'm sure your husband will be wondering where you are." Molly prodded Carol away from the deck and the man who seemed to know Steve so well.

"Why did you do that?" Carol asked once they were out of earshot. "The man was a treasure trove of information."

"What else do you need to know?" Molly shrugged. "Steve is a saint—but he could have been coming home any minute, and I didn't want to get caught." Molly's phone rang and she set Angus down to answer it as Carol unlocked the car. "Hey Bridget. Yeah, we met him. Her mom never went to the dog park. He seems like a nice guy. I think you can set Annemarie's mind at ease about him. The man doesn't even own a car, so it's not as if he could've followed her anywhere." Molly listened for a moment, then said, "Happy to help. Hopefully, Jeanette will be back by morning and all this worrying will have been for nothing."

"I'm not sure you should've said that," Carol said when Molly disconnected.

"What?"

"That you're confident Steve isn't connected to Jeanette's disappearance."

Molly's eyebrows shot up. "You think he is? Seriously?"

"Annemarie basically told me her dad lives, eats, and breathes his business—a heating and air-conditioning company."

Molly's mouth formed an *O* but no sound came out.

"That man back there said Steve's was the busiest around, so if he wasn't telling us a tall tale, it would appear that Jeanette's would-be suitor is her husband's biggest competitor. The question in my mind is, did he know who Jeanette was and deliberately bait her?"

"Or . . ." Molly cringed. "Did Jeanette know who Steve was and drum up a friendship with her husband's competition as payback?"

Carol huffed out a disbelieving breath as they both climbed into the car. "You're forgetting one important fact."

"What's that?"

Carol's heart thumped. "Jeanette is the one who's disappeared."

5

Carol rose extra early Thursday morning to help Laura replenish the bakehouse's depleted display cases. Optimistically, she first baked Jeanette's standing order of oatcakes. Would Bridget have texted if Jeanette returned home in the middle of the night? Or would she have waited, not wanting to disturb Carol's sleep?

Sleep. Carol snorted. She hadn't slept a wink, instead imagining how Steve and Mr. Franklin's business rivalry might be tied to Jeanette's disappearance. If not for her dark complexion, the telltale circles smudged under her eyes would look a whole lot worse. She glanced at the clock and saw that it was just after seven. "Do you think it's too early to text Bridget for a status report?" Carol asked Laura.

Laura set down a loaf pan of freshly baked bread. "I'm sure she won't mind."

Bridget's response came back within seconds. *Jeanette hasn't returned. Annemarie wants to come to the bakery to talk with everyone. We'll be there soon.*

Carol slipped the phone back in her pocket. "Annemarie is coming to see us again. Likely hoping we can magically divine where her mother can be found." Carol snatched up the next recipe card Laura had pulled out for her to make. "What are we supposed to do?"

Laura plopped the rolling pin she'd been using on the counter and invited Molly, who'd been filling the display cases, to join them in the kitchen. "We're going to do what we should've done yesterday. Pray."

"Trust me, I have been," Carol said.

"Me too," Molly said.

"Well, now we'll do it together." Laura reached for each of their hands.

Carol clasped Molly's other hand to close the circle. They prayed for Jeanette's well-being and that she'd come home today of her own volition, if she were able, and if not, for guidance to find her, for peace for Annemarie, and for protection from anyone who might not want her found.

Laura squeezed their hands before releasing them. "Now we wait." She picked up her rolling pin and went back to rolling out crusts for hand pies.

Admittedly, Carol felt calmed by the group prayer. The anxiety that had kept her tossing all night had been replaced with a kind of inexplicable assurance. She just hoped it wasn't false.

By the time Bridget and Annemarie arrived in the kitchen, Carol knew exactly what to tell them. "You need to go back to the police."

"That's what I was thinking too," Molly and Laura said in unison, then chuckled lightly.

"Ask them to issue a statewide BOLO on your mother's car," Carol went on.

"What's a BOLO?" Annemarie asked.

"It means 'be on the lookout,'" Carol explained.

Molly nodded. "Until we know where she parked her car, there are too many potential areas to search. If the officer you speak to refuses, I could call Greer Anderson. We're in The Piping Yoopers together," she added, referring to the town's bagpiping band. "I'm sure she'd go to bat for us."

"Good idea," Laura said, then offered more advice to Annemarie. "Ask the police to give the information to the press and to put it out on their own social media. The more people there are on the lookout for her, her car, and Scout, the better the chances of the message reaching someone with information that can help us find her."

Carol suspected the police wouldn't be ready to go as far as putting Jeanette's picture on the news given it was technically still less than twenty-four hours since she was last seen. It could prove embarrassing if Jeanette had merely treated herself to an impromptu getaway, oblivious to the worry she'd caused. Carol sucked in a deep breath. *Oh, how I hope that's all this is, that Jeanette isn't alone and hurt somewhere.*

Annemarie clung to the counter as if bracing herself against a stiff wind. Her eyes were sunken, her complexion pasty.

"We'll show your mom's picture to every single person who comes into the shop today too," Carol promised. "We'll tell them to be on the lookout for your mom, her car, and Scout. Someone has the clue to solving this mystery. I'm certain of it. We just have to find that person."

Annemarie managed to muster a shadow of a smile as she nodded. "I found a photo of her with Scout, so I printed out a stack." She held up a folder.

"That was smart," Laura said. "Did you ever connect with your aunt?"

"She called last night to talk to Jeanette," Bridget said. "She said she hasn't seen her sister in over a week and was as concerned as we were to hear she's missing."

"I'm sorry," Molly said softly, reaching out to gently squeeze Annemarie's shoulder.

Bridget checked the clock on the wall. "If it's okay with all of you, I'll go with Annemarie to the police department before starting my shift."

"Of course," Carol said as her partners also voiced agreement. "Take as long as you need."

"After I speak to the police, I'm going to drive around the area some more," Annemarie said. "I can't sit still and do nothing."

"Later this afternoon, I have to pick up an order from a printer in Beamsville," Molly said. "I can scout out all the hiking spots on the way. If she ventured farther afield than the trails on the outskirts of town, it would explain why you haven't spotted her car."

"I'll go with you," Laura offered, then glanced toward Carol.

"Me too," Carol said. "The more eyes the better, right?"

Seemingly bolstered by a fresh plan, Annemarie and Bridget left the kitchen while the Bakehouse Three returned to their business.

Two hours into serving customers, however, Carol betrayed how seriously sleep-deprived she was when she accidentally poured coffee into a customer's Scottish berry brûlée instead of the empty mug she'd set next to it. The day went from bad to worse when, just as she finished cleaning up the mess, Mr. Franklin came in.

Not knowing he was Jeanette's estranged husband, Carol showed him the picture of Jeanette and Scout, as she had every single other customer who'd come in that day. His response shocked her awake.

"What game do you think you're playing?" he demanded. "Do you know who I am?"

"No, I'm sorry." Carol shook her head. "Should I?"

He glared at her. "I'm Jack Franklin, Jeanette's husband. And I don't appreciate you flashing her picture to every Tom, Dick, and Harry who traipses through your door when for all we know, Jeanette could simply be visiting her sister."

"Have you even spoken to your daughter today, Jack?"

"It's Mr. Franklin, if you don't mind. And of course I have," he said indignantly.

"She talked to her aunt last night and reported that Karen hadn't spoken to or seen Jeanette in a week."

A little of the air went out of Mr. Franklin's puffed chest and his face reddened. "I was in the middle of a meeting. I must've missed that part."

"Trust me, Mr. Franklin," Carol said in the kindest voice she could muster despite her growing misgivings about the man. "We sincerely hope this is all a big misunderstanding and that Jeanette has simply lost her phone or something and doesn't realize how anxious Annemarie is to hear from her. But for your daughter's peace of mind, we're just trying to do everything we can to locate her mother."

Mr. Franklin gave a brisk nod, clearly reluctant to argue despite his obvious distaste for their family business being the talk of the bakery. "Appreciate it." He strode out of the bakery without ordering.

Carol's frustration with his reaction must've shown on her face, because the next person in line, Doreen, took one glimpse at her and said, "Don't pay him any mind. The man is a *bampot*."

"Yeah," Bridget chimed in, as she boxed an order for another customer. "I told you I didn't trust him."

Carol chuckled. "Do you even know what *bampot* means?"

"No," Bridget admitted. "But it doesn't sound like anything good."

"It's not," Doreen said. "It's . . ." The woman seemed to struggle to define the Scottish word.

Grizela Duff, who was born in Scotland, stood behind Doreen and cleared her throat pointedly. As the town's head librarian and president of the historical society, which taught free Gaelic lessons to interested visitors and townsfolk, she no doubt knew exactly what it meant.

Doreen spun around with a suppressed huff. "How would you define it, Grizela?"

Grizela smiled smugly. "It refers to someone who doesn't necessarily make the wisest of choices. Or who's a little unstable."

"And unlikable," Doreen added.

"That's him," Bridget muttered as she went back to her task, and Carol felt a stab of suspicion about Jeanette's estranged husband. Was he usually so brusque? Or was his mood blackened by guilt?

After lunch, Officer Michael Drummond dropped in for a

cup of coffee, and Carol asked him if the police had any leads on Jeanette's whereabouts.

The fair-skinned officer's cheeks pinked. "You know I can't talk about my cases, Mrs. MacCallan."

Carol's pulse jumped. "Her disappearance is your case?"

Officer Drummond furrowed his brow. "I didn't say that."

"You kind of did," Bridget chimed in as she passed with a bus pan of dirty dishes.

He ignored her and read aloud Laura's handwritten sign for the day's hair color special. "'For blonds only—buy six shortbread, get one free.'" He tilted his head toward the sign, unsmiling. "Mrs. MacCallan? I'm afraid I have to cite you for folliclism."

Carol blinked at him, tongue-tied.

The policeman stared solemnly back. "Folliclism," he repeated in his deep voice.

Bridget's laughter pealed out from behind Carol. "Good word."

Carol shot her a confused frown.

"Don't you get it?" Bridget asked. "Folliclism—favoritism to hair follicles of a certain color."

Carol's attention swung back to Officer Drummond. He still wore his speeding-ticket face, but now she could see there was a twinkle in his green eyes. She smiled weakly.

Bridget smirked. "I told them it wasn't fair. I'm still waiting for the free Empire biscuits on streaked-hair day."

Carol made a shooing motion toward Bridget. "You can have as many Empire biscuits as you want, and you know it."

"Mmm," Drummond said. "I might be tempted to streak my hair to get some of those." He grinned. "I'll let you off with a warning this time. But remember"—he raked his fingers through his dark red hair like a comb—"redheads like Empire biscuits too."

"Duly noted," Carol deadpanned.

By the time the shop closed, not a single tip on Jeanette's whereabouts had materialized. Bridget flipped their door sign to *Closed*, then immediately pulled her phone out of her pocket. "Annemarie texted just now," she told Carol, Molly, and Laura as they gathered around the front counter. Bridget scanned the message. "The Loch Mallaig Police Department issued the requested BOLO, but there haven't been any sightings as of yet. I'll go meet up with her as soon as we're done cleaning."

"Go ahead now," Carol told Bridget. "But does Annemarie say whether or not they've assigned an officer to Jeanette's case?"

"It's Drummond like we thought," Bridget reported, still reading over Annemarie's message. "But he didn't want to release a missing person's alert to the media this soon."

"Doesn't matter." Molly flicked her hand as if the officer's lack of cooperation was of no consequence. "One of our customers works at the local radio station, and after hearing what we were doing to try to find Jeanette, he made sure the story got on to his station's news updates. I just heard the latest."

"That's terrific," Laura said. "Now we just need somebody to call in a good tip."

While Bridget left to meet Annemarie, Molly ran upstairs to make sure Angus went out since he'd have to stay behind while the women drove the twenty miles north to Beamsville. Carol and Laura made quick work of cleaning the shop, then the three partners exited through the back door and locked it behind them.

They were just about to climb into Molly's Honda Fit when Laura gestured toward the street. An antique panel truck rumbled by with *The Artful Codger Scottish Antiques* emblazoned on its side. "Is that Henry Roberts's delivery truck?"

Molly nodded. "Cool, isn't it?"

"He must've just given it a fresh wax," Laura said. "My paint job never glows like that."

Carol snapped her fingers. "Maybe he spotted her car while out on a delivery."

"Couldn't hurt to ask," Molly said. "Besides, there's a neat slate in the window I wanted to show you two. I thought we could use it to announce the special each day."

They walked down the sidewalk, past Thistle and That, to where the delivery van was parked in front of one of Loch Mallaig's older buildings.

"Mr. Roberts really spruced up the storefront," Carol said admiringly. "I love the facade he added."

The Artful Codger continued to captivate indoors, where the women were immediately drawn in three different directions by the unusual treasures in stock, much of which was probably leftover from when Barb Nolan had run the shop as Dainty Delights. Carol was admiring a rack of hand-embroidered table linens when Laura beckoned her.

"Check out this pie safe," Laura said, directing Carol's attention toward a pine cabinet with punched-tin door inserts. She flipped over the tag. "The price isn't too shabby."

"The slate is over here," Molly called from a display near the store's cash register.

Laura and Carol walked over to where Molly was pointing out a rustic handheld chalkboard that appeared to have once been used in a one-room schoolhouse.

"Sweet." Laura ogled the find. "How much?"

"Fifteen dollars," Henry said, appearing from the back room.

Molly scrutinized the slate with a critical eye. "Will you take ten?"

"Twelve," he countered.

"Sold." Molly grinned.

Carol just hoped the purchase didn't irritate Doreen all over again. *Maybe we should pay a visit to Thistle and That to buy something and help keep the peace.*

No sooner had the thought crossed Carol's mind than Doreen appeared, coming in not through the front door, but from a side showroom. "Doreen, what a nice surprise," Carol said.

Doreen blushed. "Thought I'd check out what all the fuss is about." Her gaze drifted to the slate Henry was wrapping for them. "I guess I'd better get back to my shop. I told my assistant I wouldn't be long."

"Do you have more product upstairs?" Carol asked Henry after Doreen bustled out.

"No, just my office." Henry rang up the order, adding tax.

Molly handed him money. When the cash register drawer sprang open, it was surprisingly empty. Instead of taking change from the till, he reached into his pocket and emptied a handful of coins onto the counter, along with a small screw, a couple of washers, and a red metal dog tag.

"That's an interesting assortment of things to have in your pocket," Carol said with a laugh.

"I suppose it is. I never know what I'll find in these pockets." He counted out Molly's change, then scooped the items back into his pocket.

"Anything else I can help you ladies with?" he asked.

"Actually, yes. We're still looking for Jeanette Franklin." Carol pulled the photo of Jeanette and Scout from her purse to refresh his memory. "Have you seen her or her green Saab on any of your deliveries?"

"A green Saab?" Henry thought for a moment, then shook his head. "Not that I recall. Why?"

Carol explained Jeanette's disappearance and Henry offered to let them know if he saw anything helpful. Then, slate in hand, Molly herded them out of the shop before anything else could tempt them.

"I was surprised to see Doreen in the antiques shop," Carol said as they got settled in Molly's car.

"Well, she's not going to make me feel bad about buying a $12 slate," Molly said, shifting into gear and exiting the Bread on Arrival parking lot. "Besides, if we hadn't turned up, she might've left with a purchase or two of her own for all we know."

Having taken the passenger seat, Laura studied an area map studded with red Xs as Molly drove. "We won't be able to pass all these trailheads on our way to Beamsville or the printer will be closed before we get there."

Molly navigated onto Yooper Boulevard and headed out of town. "We can drive by some after we get the order."

Carol pulled out her phone. "I'd better text Harvey to let him know I'll be late."

They drove past five trailheads on their way to Beamsville but didn't spot any cars, let alone Jeanette's, parked along the road near them.

"Hopefully the trip back will be more fruitful," Molly said as she pulled into the printer's parking lot.

Inside, their order was ready and waiting for them. Carol and Laura took a moment to ooh and ahh over the colorful, enticing brochure that Molly had designed to advertise Bread on Arrival's website, where customers could order shortbread, cakes, cookies, and more to be shipped anywhere in the country.

"This is fantastic, Molly," Carol said.

"Yeah, you should consider a career in marketing," Laura joked.

Molly smiled at the compliments. "I had extras printed to hand out during the Scottish Games festival later this month. We're supposed to get thousands of visitors, and tons of them from far away. This way, they'll know they can get our goodies no matter where they live."

Laura winked. "That's our Molly, always thinking."

As they headed toward the exit, Carol suddenly realized they hadn't taken the opportunity to show the shopkeeper Jeanette's picture. She returned to the counter and held out the photo, giving the same spiel she'd repeated all day. "You wouldn't happen to have seen this woman around town today or yesterday, would you?"

The older woman put on her reading glasses and studied Jeanette's face. Removing her glasses, she said, "Sorry. Can't say I have."

"Have you heard about or seen a stray springer spaniel in the area?" Molly asked.

The woman frowned and shook her head. "The woman is missing, I take it? And had a dog with her?"

"That's right," Laura said.

"Does she happen to drive a green Saab?"

"Yes!" the trio exclaimed at once, and Carol asked, "Have you seen it?"

"No," the clerk said. "But the customer before you said a tow truck was pulling one out of the ditch on Torrent Street."

"Where's that?" Molly asked.

The shopkeeper gave them directions. "If the tow truck is already gone, he'll probably tow it to the impound lot across from the sheriff's station on Fifth."

The women thanked her for the help, then rushed to the car. Molly followed the clerk's directions, turning onto Torrent just as the tow truck driver was circling the now-secured car to check the cables.

Molly parked behind the tow truck, and Carol jumped out just as the driver was opening the cab door.

"Excuse me," Carol said, waving to get the man's attention. "Could you tell me where the driver of this car is?"

"Nope." The man paused with his hand on the door handle, his shirt sleeve falling back to reveal a cascade of tattoos down his arm. He scrutinized Carol a moment, then added, "The sheriff sent me to haul it out of the ditch. No one was around when I got here."

Carol winced, thinking Jeanette must have been injured and taken to the hospital . . . if this was her car. "Did you happen to see a stray dog around?"

"Nah. No dog." The man opened the door and hefted himself up to the seat.

"Wait!" Molly called as she and Laura joined Carol. "We think this is our friend's car. She's been missing since yesterday. May we check the paperwork in the glove box before you go? Please?" Molly adopted a pleading expression, which Laura and Carol mirrored.

"I don't think so." The man stared down at them from his perch, bristling with impatience.

"It'll only take a minute," Molly pressed.

"Sorry. It's against the rules." The driver slammed his door, not sounding the least bit apologetic.

Laura raced to the front of the truck and planted herself there.

He scrutinized his side mirror, but Molly's car was parked too close for him to back up and go around. "Move it, lady," he groused through his open window.

Laura defiantly crossed her arms in front of her chest. "Not until you let us check the glove box."

"Suit yourself." The man fired up his engine and noisily worked the gears. It appeared as though he and the Bakehouse Three were locked in a game of chicken.

And he didn't intend to lose.

6

Carol gasped as the tow truck lurched menacingly toward Laura.

But Laura scarcely flinched.

His bluff called, the tow truck driver braked and stuck his head out his side window. "Are you nuts, lady?" he hollered.

"Come on." Molly smiled sweetly. "Who's it going to hurt if we glance at the name on the registration?"

The man scowled at Laura, then said, "Fine. Check the glove box. But be quick about it."

Carol climbed onto the flatbed. From the looks of it, the car had landed on its right side in the ditch. The passenger's side door was crushed in, and remnants of the exploded windshield littered the front seats, which were otherwise empty. There was no purse or phone. Carol reached through the open passenger window to check the glove box. Inside was a folded plastic sleeve people often used for their registration and insurance cards. Carol took a deep breath and withdrew the documents inside.

"It's Jeanette's car," she announced to the others, then returned the paperwork to the glove box before climbing off the flatbed.

Laura waited until Carol was safely down on the ground before stepping out of the tow truck's path.

"Thanks for helping us out," Molly called up to the driver as he made a production of grinding his gears.

"Yeah, sure," he muttered and lurched away.

"Way to go, Laura!" Molly hugged her. "That was quick thinking."

Laura beamed. "I saw it in a movie once. I'm just glad it worked. But now I think I need to sit down for a minute."

Smiling at her courage, Carol and Molly guided their friend back to the car.

"Where to first?" Molly asked, buckling her seat belt. "The hospital or the sheriff's?"

"The sheriff's," Carol said.

"You should call Annemarie," Laura said to Carol as Molly turned the car toward the station.

Carol almost reached for her phone, then had second thoughts. "Let's wait until we hear what the sheriff has to say."

When they told the receptionist at the sheriff's office they were there to inquire about the green Saab that had been in an accident on Torrent, Sheriff Lon Bugle himself ushered them into his office. The burly man with salt-and-pepper mutton chops motioned them to his office's visitor seats, then planted his hip on the corner of his desk. "What can you ladies tell me about that abandoned Saab?"

"It was abandoned?" Laura asked, shooting a worried glance toward Molly and Carol. "I've heard of people losing their memory in a car crash. If she's got a head injury, Jeanette could be wandering around here somewhere, not knowing who or where she is."

"You're talking about Jeanette Franklin, the car's owner?" Sheriff Bugle clarified.

"Yes," Carol answered. "She hasn't been seen or heard from since yesterday morning, and her daughter is very worried."

The sheriff nodded. "I've tried several times to reach Mrs. Franklin at the number listed with the DMV."

"Did anyone see the accident?" Molly asked. "Do you know what happened?"

"No." The sheriff crossed his arms. "The car was abandoned in the ditch. A deputy noticed it a few hours ago and conducted a preliminary search of the vehicle and surroundings. We don't believe Mrs. Franklin was the driver though."

"Why not?" Carol asked in surprise.

"The steering column had been hot-wired," Bugle explained. "I suspect the would-be car thief crashed it in the wee hours of the morning while joyriding about the countryside. There was no sign of blood in the car, so he likely ran off after the crash, not wanting to be caught with a stolen vehicle."

"Then where's Jeanette?" Laura voiced the question haunting Carol.

The sheriff gritted his teeth. "It's not common in these parts, but it's possible our thief took the car by force and left her injured wherever she'd been parked. I did check with our local hospital and they had no Jeanettes or Jane Does meeting her description admitted in the last twenty-four hours. What is the last known location you have for her?"

Carol gave him a rundown of all they knew and the places they'd checked, then asked, "Do you suspect someone in particular? Or did you lift prints from the car to see if you could get a match?"

"We lifted a couple of clear prints and are running them through the system," Sheriff Bugle said. "But I'm afraid that doesn't work as quickly as you'd think."

"Are you going to issue a press release?" Molly asked. "And you should really get in touch with the Loch Mallaig police."

"We absolutely will," he reassured her. "If we get lucky, someone might turn in the thief and he can tell us where he found the car."

A short while later, Sheriff Bugle escorted them out with a promise to keep in touch.

"Well, there's no point checking out more trailheads now," Laura said as they walked to the parking lot. "Back to Loch Mallaig?"

"I think that's best," Molly said. "Just in case the sheriff doesn't contact our local police right away, we need to bring them up to speed on Jeanette's situation."

"I should touch base with Bridget so she can update Annemarie." Carol dialed Bridget's number, and the girl answered on the first ring. "Are you with Annemarie?" Carol asked.

"She's right here. Let me put you on speaker," Bridget said. "Did you find her mom's car?"

"Yes, but we're just not sure if it's good or bad." Carol filled the girls in on what they knew so far. She winced at the sound of Annemarie sniffling in the background. "We're on our way back to town and plan to update Officer Drummond as soon as we get there. I don't see how he could not act on the case now."

"We're only a few minutes away," Molly announced when Carol ended the call. "How'd Annemarie take the news?"

"Not well," Carol said. "She's going to try to reach her dad now."

Laura clucked sympathetically. "Poor thing."

Carol checked her watch. "Hopefully Officer Drummond hasn't already left for the day."

After parking, the trio hurried into the police station. Wilma perked up at the sight of them. She spoke rapidly into the cell phone that always seemed to be glued to her ear, then set it down. "How can I help you girls?" she asked brightly even though she had only a few years on them.

"We'd like to speak to Michael Drummond if he's in," Laura said.

Wilma patted her poufy red hair. "Is this about Jeanette Franklin?"

Carol's heart thumped. "Did the Beamsville sheriff call here about her car?"

Surprise flickered in Wilma's bright blue eyes. "No, not that I've heard." She leaned forward intently, inviting more information.

Carol bit her lip, wishing she hadn't jumped to conclusions.

Wilma had no doubt heard about their showing Jeanette's picture to every customer today and likely assumed they were there to pressure Drummond into doing more to find Jeanette.

"Did the Beamsville sheriff's department spot Jeanette's car?" Wilma pressed eagerly.

"Time is of the essence here," Laura said, her tone firm. "Is Officer Drummond in?"

Carol couldn't blame her friend for being terse. Truth be told, she was grateful. Wilma was nice enough, but she loved to gossip—or *blether,* as Hamish liked to call it—especially on the phone. She liked to say it was in her DNA as a descendant of Alexander Graham Bell. But they didn't have time to waste being quizzed by her when they needed to be updating Michael Drummond on what they'd learned so he could act on the information.

Wilma sighed but picked up the phone to announce their arrival. A moment later, Officer Drummond greeted them warmly at the front desk.

Carol relaxed, relieved by his willingness to hear what they had to say.

He escorted the women down the hall and into the bullpen, where his desk was situated among a handful of others. He pulled two extra chairs over and invited them to sit across from him while he took a seat. "Wilma said you have news about Mrs. Franklin's car?"

All three women started to speak at once, and Officer Drummond raised his hand. "One at a time, please." He pointed to Molly. "How about you start?"

Molly explained how they'd found the tow truck loading Jeanette's abandoned car and had checked the registration in the glove box to confirm it was hers. Laura continued by filling him in on their conversation with the Beamsville sheriff.

"He should have called you by now, so maybe you should call him," Carol concluded. "He may already know who stole the vehicle." When Drummond continued writing the details they'd relayed in his notepad without seeming to acknowledge her suggestion, Carol added, "Clearly something must've happened to Jeanette. Otherwise, she would have reported her car stolen."

Officer Drummond nodded. "Rest assured that I will contact Sheriff Bugle." He rose, apparently planning to escort them out before making the call.

Carol's chest tightened. Who knew what other emergency might erupt and pull him away from his desk before he could follow through on his promise? "If it's okay," she said politely, "we'll wait here while you call him."

As if he understood her concern, Drummond nodded and picked up his desk phone.

"We should launch a search party immediately," Molly murmured to the other women while Officer Drummond spoke to the sheriff.

But he must have overheard her because after he hung up the phone, he said, "Until we determine where Jeanette Franklin's car was stolen from, we have no idea where to start searching. There are too many square miles of forest between Loch Mallaig and Beamsville, not to mention in any other direction Jeanette might've headed yesterday morning."

"We have to do *something*," Laura said, her voice equal parts pleading, anguish, and insistence. Before joining Molly and Carol in Loch Mallaig to open Bread on Arrival, Laura had last worked as a chef in NYC, and Carol suspected that while there, she'd heard of too many carjackings gone wrong.

"I will get the pictures of Jeanette, her car, and her dog that Annemarie gave me to the Upper Michigan news stations with the updated information and a request for tips." He glanced at the clock on the wall. "It's past six, so it won't likely be broadcast until the late news."

"It could run sooner if you call right now," Molly urged.

Drummond acknowledged this with a nod and turned to his computer. Within minutes, he had sent the images through to the news station. "Okay, the photos are on their way. I'll follow up with a phone call, then I need to go to the Franklin house to see if I can lift samples of Jeanette's prints to eliminate them from those taken from the car."

"I'll go too," Carol volunteered. "News of finding her mom's stolen car has really upset Annemarie, and I'd like to reassure her there's still hope."

"If you'd like." This time when the policeman stood, he urged them all out of their chairs. "I'd appreciate it if you excuse me while I make the calls." He escorted them to the hallway and they made their own way outside.

"Molly and I can start organizing a search party," Laura offered. "We can narrow down the search area after they run the photos on the news, assuming some valid tips come in."

"That's a terrific idea," Carol said. "Annemarie will be encouraged to hear you're doing it."

A gleaming silver Range Rover pulled to the curb beside them and the passenger side window opened. A ruggedly handsome man with a neatly-trimmed dark beard leaned across from the driver's seat and smiled at them.

"Hello, ladies." An extra twinkle sparkled in Fergus MacGregor's blue eyes as his gaze alighted on Molly. The pair had been good friends as teens when Molly's family had vacationed in Loch Mallaig, and their friendship had picked up naturally upon Molly's recent move to town. "Anything new with the search for Jeanette Franklin?"

"How much time do you have?" Laura asked wryly.

"As much as you need," Fergus said, then parked his car and joined them on the sidewalk. Molly, Carol, and Laura filled Fergus in on what they knew, then shared their theories of what might have happened to Jeanette.

"Bridget fears the woman's ex had something to do with her disappearance," Laura added at the end.

Fergus shook his head. "Not a chance. First of all, the Franklins aren't divorced yet. Jack is still trying to win Jeanette back. He's been an emotional wreck since they separated."

"How do you know him?" Carol asked.

"He's a longtime member of Castleglen." Fergus was the third-generation owner of the prestigious golf club, lodge, and resort.

Given the Franklins' wealth, Carol shouldn't have been surprised Jack Franklin was a member, except that . . . "I had the impression he was an all work and no play kind of guy."

"That's exactly what caused the split," Fergus told them. "The only time he plays golf is to entertain clients when trying to secure major deals. But he supplies most of the business and apartment complexes in the Upper Peninsula with climate controls systems, so he entertains a fair bit."

"You said he's trying to win Jeanette back?" Molly repeated. "Is it possible he lost it with her in a fit of frustration when she refused to listen to his pleas?"

"Not this week," Fergus said. "He knew she wouldn't change her mind until he could prove he'd stop working eighty hours a week. That's why he's in negotiations with a national conglomerate to sell his company." Fergus scratched his beard. "From what I hear, the negotiations have been intense. I doubt he's had time to even try to see his wife in the past week."

"His competition—I mean the smaller mom-and-pop operations—must not be too happy about his pending deal," Molly said.

"It seems every time a national firm worms in on a local market share, it isn't long before they eliminate the competition."

"The sale could hurt smaller operations, for sure," Fergus agreed. "Right now they can make a decent go of it with residential installations and maintenance, but once Jack's company is taken over by the bigger one, it'll have the volume to demand huge wholesale discounts from suppliers. Discounts that could easily squeeze the smaller players out of the sales market, leaving them to try and survive doing maintenance almost exclusively."

Carol's thoughts turned to Steve the sheltie owner, who'd somehow managed to slip her mind until now. The fact he owned a company in direct competition to Jack Franklin's couldn't be a coincidence, could it? "Do you think a competitor would go as far as kidnapping Mr. Franklin's wife to disrupt the negotiations?"

Fergus chuckled. "I doubt it. A small-town operator wouldn't risk felony charges on an exploit that isn't likely to change the outcome in the long run."

Molly tapped her chin. "Unless he also plans to swoop in and beat Franklin to the sale."

Laura shook her head. "You're forgetting one thing. His wife's disappearance hasn't distracted Mr. Franklin one iota from his negotiations."

"Maybe not yet," Molly said.

"Because he could still convince himself she merely went away without telling anyone," Carol added. "But now that her *stolen* car has been found with no sign of her . . ."

Fergus shook his head solemnly. "Things are about to get a whole lot messier."

7

As unlikely as it was that her car would have been missing, Carol breathed a sigh of relief when she saw the white Chrysler still parked in the lot at Bread on Arrival. Before this afternoon, the notion of someone stealing it would never have crossed her mind. Then again, chances were that Jeanette's car hadn't been nicked from Loch Mallaig. But it had been too close to their town for comfort.

Laura elbowed Carol as they waited for Molly to unlock the bakery door. "I think I'll ride along with you to the Franklins' house."

"What about recruiting volunteers?" Carol asked.

"Fergus offered to help Molly, and three's a crowd." Laura wore a knowing smirk.

"You two can get going," Molly said over her shoulder. "Fergus will be here in a minute. You don't want to keep Officer Drummond waiting."

"Have fun with Fergus," Laura sang out as she sauntered toward Carol's car. Molly pointedly ignored her and disappeared into the bakehouse with the antique slate and her brochures.

"Are you playing matchmaker?" Carol teased as she backed out of the driveway.

Laura shrugged. "If they spend a little more time alone together, maybe they'll both realize what's pretty obvious to the rest of us."

"What's that?"

"The old spark is still there."

"Mmhmm." As she drove to Annemarie's house, Carol's thoughts drifted to Harvey. She couldn't imagine life without him. But Molly had already lost a husband. The pain of grieving his death had to prey on her mind at the prospect of rekindling romantic feelings for Fergus.

Officer Drummond's cruiser was already parked in front of the Franklin home when Carol and Laura arrived. He climbed out of his vehicle to meet them on the front walkway.

Bridget didn't seem surprised to see the police officer with her bosses when she opened the door. Instead, she merely gestured for them to come inside. "We can go in the great room. Annemarie will be out in a minute."

Laura's jaw dropped as she stepped into the impressive living space. "Wow. Jeanette is so down-to-earth and unpretentious. I never would've guessed she lives like this."

"I get the sense from Annemarie that her mom isn't all that enamored with the trappings," Carol murmured.

Laura went to the window and admired the picturesque view of the lake. "Then again, you can't get much closer to nature than this."

Annemarie entered the room, her eyes red-rimmed and bloodshot. "Hello, officer."

"Miss Franklin, I'm sorry to trouble you," Officer Drummond said. "I know this discovery is distressing. But we need to eliminate your mom's prints from the ones the sheriff in Beamsville lifted from her car."

Annemarie nodded dully.

"Your mom's hairbrush or maybe her perfume bottle might be the best objects to try dusting for prints," Drummond suggested, his tone gentle.

After a long pause, as if the words took some time to sink in, Annemarie pointed toward the staircase. "My parents'—my mom's bedroom is upstairs." The urgency that had marked her tone the day before had given way to resignation, and Carol wondered if the poor girl was in shock.

Annemarie led Officer Drummond away, leaving the rest of them standing in the great room.

"I don't know what to say to her," Bridget admitted. "Her dad didn't even take her call when she tried to reach him. I want to help keep up her spirits, but I don't want to give her false hope. Do you know what I mean?"

Carol squeezed her shoulder. "You're here for her. That's what matters."

Hugging herself, Laura shook her head. "I can scarcely imagine what the poor thing must be going through. It's just too horrible." Laura paced the room. "There's nothing here to indicate where she liked to hike?"

Bridget pointed to a trail map book lying atop the antique table Carol had admired the day before. "We found that. It's pretty dog-eared, and Annemarie had already checked the trailheads of every trail with a page corner turned down."

"Jeanette's car could've already been stolen by then," Carol said grimly.

"Have you seen this?" Laura interrupted, examining the table the trail map book sat on. "Something like this would look great in the bakery by the fireplace, don't you think?"

"Yes, Molly thought the same," Carol admitted. "It's from The Artful Codger."

Laura's eyes brightened. "We definitely need to browse that shop some more."

"Except Doreen sells accent tables too. Do you really want to invite her ire by buying one from Henry?"

"Mr. Roberts is a regular Bread on Arrival customer too. Why shouldn't we support his business?" Bridget argued.

"Exactly!" Laura said. "Besides, Doreen only carries a couple of styles of accent tables. I know because I've already checked them out."

Laura moved on to the bookcase to admire a stunning sculpture of a snowy owl, one of several different pieces in Jeanette's owl collection. Carol's favorite was the painting over the sofa of an owl that appeared as if it was having a particularly bad hair day.

Carol motioned toward the large TV. "Do you think Annemarie would mind if we turn that on? There's still a few minutes left in the news and I'd like to see if the picture of Jeanette made it into the broadcast."

"Oh of course." Bridget picked up the remote control and tuned the TV to the local station. "Annemarie will want to know too."

Sure enough, the all-too-familiar image of Jeanette and Scout filled half the screen as the newscaster entreated anyone who had seen them in the last thirty-six hours to call the number shown.

Carol hadn't registered the return of Annemarie and Officer Drummond, and she startled when Annemarie burst into fresh tears. Bridget put her arm around her friend as they watched the rest of the newscast. A moment later, the photo of Jeanette and Scout faded and was replaced by a picture of Jeanette's green Saab, this one taken before the passenger's side had been smashed in and the windshield shattered. Carol sent up a prayer of gratitude for that small mercy. Her mother's smashed car, even if Jeanette hadn't been driving it at the time, was the last thing Annemarie needed to see right now.

As soon as the newscaster signed off, Officer Drummond raised his hand in farewell to the rest of them. "I have all I need for now. I'll be in touch as soon as I have more information."

Carol helped Annemarie walk him out to the front porch, if only for something to do. Carol watched the cruiser glide down the driveway, racking her brain for something she could say that might offer encouragement and much needed hope. But before she had the opportunity to talk to Annemarie, Mr. Franklin roared up to the house in his sleek BMW.

Carol's first thought was uncharitable if not unfounded. *Isn't it interesting how he found time to take his car for a wash and wax but couldn't break from his meetings to answer his hurting daughter's phone call?* With a sigh, she reminded herself that a man in his position likely had an assistant who took care of such menial tasks as having his car detailed.

The graphite-hued BMW ground to a halt and Mr. Franklin stepped out. "What were the police doing here?" he demanded, his tone terse.

Annemarie bounded down the porch steps and flung herself into her father's arms. "You're here!"

But by the look of the check envelope he held in his hand, Mr. Franklin hadn't been thinking of her as much as fulfilling the terms of his separation agreement with his wife. Namely, delivering a weekly support check.

The force of his daughter's embrace clearly caught him by surprise, but his rigidity melted away as he hugged her back. "What's going on, pumpkin?" he asked gently. "Are you still worried about your mother?"

"They found her car, Dad," Annemarie sobbed against his shoulder. "It was stolen and then abandoned way out in Beamsville."

Mr. Franklin stiffened at the news.

"But Mom never reported it stolen," Annemarie went on, lifting her head to gaze pleadingly into his eyes, silently begging him to fix it. "Something's happened to her. I know it. No one has seen Mom or Scout anywhere."

Mr. Franklin gently rocked his daughter. His expression, if it could be believed, suggested he was visibly shaken by his daughter's distress or over his wife's seemingly dire situation.

Carol hurried down the stairs to offer what moral support she could.

But before she reached them, Mr. Franklin seemed to recover himself. "I'm sure it's all a misunderstanding, pumpkin," he said. "Your mom probably went away with your aunt somewhere and doesn't even know her car is missing."

Carol stopped short, her hands fisted at her sides, and inwardly fumed that the man was too thick to remember their earlier conversation.

"No, Daddy. Remember?" Annemarie pulled back. "Aunt Karen hasn't heard from her either."

He clasped Annemarie's shoulders and searched her eyes. "Well, I'm sure your mother will be back by tomorrow. Because that's when she was expecting you home." He chucked her chin affectionately.

"No, Daddy. You're not listening."

He stiffened once more, but this time his irritation was obvious. "What I know is that crying won't help anyone. Chin up, now."

Carol hovered nearby, debating whether to intervene. Absently, she glanced into Mr. Franklin's car. Muddy paw prints covered the leather back seat and she suddenly grew skeptical about what he'd seemed so shaken about a few moments ago. Maybe that the discovery of his wife's car was pushing the investigation too close for comfort. "What kind of dog do you have, Mr. Franklin?" she asked.

"Excuse me, who are you?" he asked sharply.

"This is Carol MacCallan," Annemarie said, drying her eyes. "She's one of the women who found Mom's car."

Mr. Franklin extended his hand and thanked her, not seeming to recognize her from their earlier conversation at Bread on Arrival. Did an apron change her appearance that much? Or was he just that distracted?

The man's handshake was clammy and limp, not at all the kind of handshake she'd expect from a successful businessman.

But maybe it was the kind she should expect from someone wary about having a secret found out.

"Do you have a dog, Mr. Franklin?" Carol pressed. "Because I couldn't help but notice the paw prints on your car's back seat."

"No way!" Annemarie shifted to peer in the window. "Dad hates pets of any kind."

"That's not true," he protested. "I was okay with your goldfish."

"That's because he was in my room and you never saw him." She squinted up at her dad. "So where'd all the paw prints come from?"

"That ridiculous mutt your mom adopted the instant I moved out jumps into my car every chance he gets."

Carol held her breath, waiting for Annemarie to verify her father's claim.

Annemarie studied her father in silence for an uncomfortably long moment. Did she think he was lying? He'd obviously just had the car's exterior cleaned. It seemed odd he wouldn't have the interior detailed at the same time. Then again, if he'd had something to hide, wouldn't he have ensured all traces of dog hair and paw prints were erased?

Finally, Annemarie nodded. "It's true. For some inexplicable reason, Scout does adore you."

Mr. Franklin rolled his eyes. "My assistant forgot to have my interior detailed, so the prints are still there from last week."

Carol didn't want to think the worst of Annemarie's father, but she also wasn't ready to dismiss the paw prints on his back seat as inconsequential to the investigation. How could she ask him questions without it sounding like an interrogation?

Laura and Bridget joined them in the driveway. "Mr. Franklin, I'm Laura Donovan." Laura extended her hand as she introduced herself. "I own Bread on Arrival with Carol and our friend Molly, who's currently working with Fergus MacGregor to organize a search party."

Mr. Franklin shook her hand and grunted a greeting, but he perked up when she mentioned Fergus.

"Right now, Molly and Fergus are calling everyone we know from church, local businesses and organizations, and even friends of friends to join in a search for your wife tomorrow morning. We're confident someone will remember seeing her car after tonight's news report."

"News report?" Mr. Franklin repeated in confusion.

"Finding Mom's car finally convinced the police she's really missing," Annemarie explained. "That's why Officer Drummond was here."

"But I'm sure whoever took her car didn't actually confront your mom," Bridget said assuredly, clearly trying her best to shore up her friend's hopes. "Car thieves tend to be opportunists. Right, Carol?"

"From what I hear, yes." To Mr. Franklin, Carol added, "But in addition to being left stranded by her car going missing, your wife might've suffered an injury that's left her unable to walk. That could be why she hasn't appeared seeking help."

Mr. Franklin groaned. "I wish she would've listened to me and given up that old Saab years ago. If she drove a new car like mine, we could've tracked its location from the moment Annemarie started to worry."

Carol couldn't help but wonder if its ability to be tracked was exactly why Jeanette had declined a state-of-the-art car. "Can you track her phone?"

"Theoretically, yes," Mr. Franklin said. "But she turned off location services and data, so no. Besides, it's an old phone so the battery is probably dead." He sighed in frustration. "Another relic she wouldn't give up."

"I can't believe I didn't think of it sooner." Laura slapped a palm to her forehead and everyone turned toward her. "My brother's friend, Toby, has a small Cessna. I'm sure he'd be willing to fly over the peninsula to see if we can spot anything from the sky."

"Maybe Mrs. Franklin was able to start a signal fire," Bridget interjected encouragingly.

Laura pulled out her phone. "I'll call Toby right now."

As everyone watched Laura make the call, Carol formulated another question for Annemarie's father—one that wouldn't sound accusatory, she hoped. "You didn't see your wife at all yesterday morning?"

He shook his head. "I'm not her favorite person these days. I'm sure my daughter told you we're currently separated."

"Yes. I'm sorry," Carol said.

"It's my own fault." He absently watched a squirrel scurry across the driveway and up a chestnut tree. "I work too much. In fact, I've been in nonstop meetings since first thing yesterday morning."

Carol frowned. His meetings hadn't been *entirely* nonstop, given his appearance at the bakery that morning. "The meetings were at your office?"

"Between meals, yes."

So presumably there would be employees who could verify his alibi, Carol thought but didn't dare say out loud.

Mr. Franklin squeezed his daughter's hand. "I'm sorry I was abrupt with you when you called and stopped by. I was in the middle of a critical point in the negotiation. But the deal is supposed to close tomorrow morning. And if it goes the way I hope, I will have all the time in the world to spend with your mom."

If she's still alive. Carol shivered as the words hung in the air, unspoken but likely thought by everyone present.

Mr. Franklin gave his daughter's arm a gentle tug. "Come home with me." He glanced around the sheltered yard, scarcely visible from the street or by neighbors thanks to the trees. "I don't like you being here alone like this. I'll call the police and insist they step up whatever they're doing to find your mother."

Annemarie pulled her hand from his grasp. "No, Dad. I don't want to stay at your depressing apartment. I want to be here in case Mom calls or comes back." She started for the house.

"She's not alone, Mr. Franklin," Bridget said, trailing her friend. "I'm staying the night with her."

"That's nice of you, Bridget. I think I'll stay too," he said.

Annemarie stopped in her tracks, her face brightening just the slightest bit. "I'd like that."

Mr. Franklin nodded once. "It's settled then. I'll just go pick up an overnight bag. And I can grab a pizza on the way back. Sound good?"

"Sure. Thanks, Dad." With a half-hearted wave, Annemarie disappeared into the house with Bridget. She was clearly exhausted by the unrelenting stress of her mother's disappearance.

"I don't like the idea of the girls being here alone," Mr. Franklin said to Carol and Laura. "Especially if, God forbid, Jeanette was the victim of foul play." He shuddered. "My wife always preferred to explore the roads less traveled. I can't tell you how many times I pleaded with her to stick to well-used trails on her hikes. As much as I dislike dogs, it was actually a relief when she adopted one after she kicked me out. I figured at least she wouldn't be hiking alone." He drew in a deep breath and expelled it slowly, his expression pained. "Who knows what she could have stumbled on out there in the woods?"

"I wouldn't speculate in front of your daughter," Carol told him. "Her imagination is wild enough."

He nodded solemnly, then pulled a business card from his wallet and held it out. "Please, call me as soon as you've determined a search area. I want to be there."

"Of course." Laura grabbed the card and pocketed it. "My friend with the seaplane is picking me up here in a few minutes. Hopefully your wife has managed to move into the open or to start a signal fire we can spot."

"Yes." Mr. Franklin's voice cracked as he opened his car door. "Thank you."

Carol rushed forward before he could leave. "Mr. Franklin, is it possible a rival company might've kidnapped your wife to distract you from your business meetings?"

A tremble in his cheek muscle was the only indication the question might've rattled him. "It's unlikely. It's no secret my wife and I have been separated for months."

Laura raised an eyebrow. "But I suspect it's also no secret that you still love her deeply. Yes?"

He blinked rapidly, as if forcing back tears. "I don't know what I'd do if something happened to her. I know she probably doesn't believe it these days, but I'd be lost without her. I am lost without her." He cleared his throat and shrugged off the emotional admission. "But I doubt my competitors know me that well."

He climbed into the car and slammed the door, then started the engine and took off down the driveway like a rocket.

"He seems genuinely concerned about his wife's welfare," Laura said, watching the BMW fishtail slightly as Mr. Franklin backed onto the street and speed away. "Even if he's trying to take out his aggression on his accelerator."

Carol chewed on her bottom lip, her stomach churning as she mulled over his possible motivations. "I can't help wondering if the reason he wants to stay with Annemarie is to somehow cover his tracks."

8

When she returned home that evening to find Harvey out fishing, Carol phoned Officer Drummond and floated the idea that Jeanette might've stumbled on to something nefarious in the woods.

"It's more likely she merely stumbled," the officer reassured her.

Carol released an audible sigh.

"I know the waiting is difficult, Mrs. MacCallan. But we are making progress. I spoke with Sheriff Bugle. The fingerprints lifted from Jeanette's steering wheel belong to a young man known to police for assault and battery. A warrant has already been issued for his arrest."

Carol's heart crunched at the offenses on the suspect's rap sheet, and she silently prayed for Jeanette's safety.

"Unfortunately," Drummond went on, "he was evicted three weeks ago from the address on file. But the sheriff's department has a couple of deputies out looking for him."

"Do they know where he works? They could pick him up there."

"I'm sure they've thought of that." A hint of impatience colored Drummond's tone. He took a deep breath before continuing. "I suspect the eviction might mean he's between jobs. But don't worry. Sheriff Bugle runs a tight ship, and his deputies are well trained."

"Did any tips come in from the news broadcast yet?" Carol asked.

"Only one, but it was for a different green Saab still parked where the caller had spotted it the previous day."

Stifling a groan, Carol thanked the officer for his efforts before hanging up. Feeling a visceral need to stay busy, she checked in with Molly and Fergus to find out how the volunteer list was coming.

"We've rounded up an impressive number of searchers," Molly said. "Fergus got volunteers from Castleglen, both members and staff. Everyone is meeting at Bread on Arrival at eight."

"That's fantastic." After chatting a little while longer, Carol said goodbye to Molly then continued to putter aimlessly as dusk fell, dusting already spotless shelves and shooting occasional glances out the window for signs of Harvey returning from his fishing trip. Although she didn't stop moving, the cozy log-style house was quiet and peaceful, so the sudden ringing of the landline made her jump. She hurried to the kitchen and picked up the receiver. "Hello?"

Laura was on the other end of the line, excitement brimming in her voice. "Toby and I spotted smoke from two campfires and reported the coordinates to police. They're going in with four-wheelers to investigate."

A rush of hope coursed through Carol. "That's promising."

"Do you think I should call Mr. Franklin to let him know?"

"As much as I want to keep the Franklins up to speed, we don't want to get Annemarie's hopes up unnecessarily," Carol said. "If the police find Jeanette, I'm sure Annemarie will be the first person they call."

Harvey returned home just as Carol was hanging up the phone after her chat with Laura. Once Carol had shared the latest, he attempted to take her mind off her concerns by putting on a movie. But an hour into the film, she couldn't stand the suspense any longer. She called Officer Drummond to ask about the search for the campfires.

"Both fires turned out to be youth gatherings," the policeman said, sounding as disappointed as she felt. "But more tips are coming in now that the late news is running the story and pictures again. Once we weed out the obvious dead ends, we should be able to narrow in on a few viable leads."

"That's great," Carol said, then told him about the volunteers ready to hit the trails the next morning to search for Jeanette. She felt her strength renewed as she figured out how she could channel her nervous energy. "If you could give me the list of locations people have spotted either the car or Jeanette and Scout, we'll log them on a map, then we can work out how to divide the searchers."

"Good idea, but I've got to warn you," Drummond said. "At this point, the tips are vastly contradictory, putting Jeanette's car parked simultaneously near forests on opposite ends of the county. But given there are a handful of green Saabs registered to drivers in the Upper Peninsula, not to mention likely a tourist or two, the tips could all be legitimate, just not about Jeanette's green Saab. Unfortunately, it's too late now to call people, but I'll have my men call the other registered owners at first light to find out where their cars were parked Wednesday. That should help us eliminate some of the options."

"Perfect. Did anyone claim to actually see Jeanette and Scout?"

Drummond sighed heavily before delivering his answer. "No."

Carol's heart fell at the news, but she steeled herself against getting too discouraged. Jeanette had to be out there somewhere. All they had to do was find her.

Although Carol was accustomed to waking before dawn to get to the bakehouse, she rose even earlier the next morning. Unable to go back to the movie after Officer Drummond's phone call, Harvey had dug through his office and found a large folded map of the tri-county area he'd gotten at the chamber of commerce, then helped Carol pin it to a large corkboard. She had added red pins at Jeanette's house and Beamsville, where her car had been found, and planned to add more based on the tips that came through the tip line.

She studied the map for a few minutes that morning, thinking hard about the strategy for their search, then went out to the chicken coop. Even the hens' boisterous clucks and feather ruffling at the appearance of breakfast didn't distract her from the task ahead.

When she emerged from the coop with that morning's collection of eggs, Harvey was loading the bulletin board into her car. He closed the door and caught sight of her, offering that reflexive smile that always came to his face when he saw his wife. "I've rounded up a few of my fishing buddies to help with the search," he said. "I told them to meet at the bakery at eight."

"That's very helpful, honey," Carol said, appreciating his supportive gesture. "Thank you."

"I was thinking I could go in with you now, though," he said as he joined her near the house. "With so many people showing up at the bakehouse, you ladies are going to need a lot of extra product on hand. If you want to help Laura and Molly with that, I'd be happy to take the map to the police station and populate it."

"Why, do you have experience with that sort of thing?" Carol teased. Harvey's decades of investigative reporting had honed many helpful skills.

Harvey shrugged. "A little."

Carol patted his cheek. "Have I told you how much I love you?"

"Not as much as I love you. I'm so proud of how you and your friends have pulled the community together to search for this missing woman."

With a sigh, Carol carried the egg basket to the back door. "I just hope it's not too little too late." She opened the door and walked through, then held it for Harvey. "If we'd been able to get the information on the news the first night, we might've found her by now."

Harvey made toast while Carol fried up the morning's haul of eggs for breakfast. Consenting to living in a log cabin on the lake in exchange for his support of her business venture had been no hardship. She loved listening to the call of the loons at night and indulging in fresh eggs every morning. But today all she could do was worry whether or not Jeanette was injured and fret about when she'd had anything to eat, or when her last dose of insulin had been. She didn't know much about type 1 diabetes, but she knew those who had it needed to balance their carbohydrates carefully with their insulin or risk nasty consequences.

Harvey gently nudged Carol aside and took the eggs off the heat.

Carol realized she'd let them cook longer than either of them preferred. "Sorry, I was thinking of Jeanette. Being diabetic is hard enough in civilization. Who knows how she's faring out in the wilderness . . . if that's where she is."

"At least you know she always carries your oatcakes with her, so she had something to eat."

"Her last order was a week ago. Besides, even if she had some, they wouldn't be enough to satisfy her appetite this long. And the mosquitoes are brutal out there this morning."

Harvey nodded. "I noticed them when I came in from fishing last night. But people have survived a lot worse." He dished the eggs and toast onto plates and set them on the table. "You've got to have faith." Taking her hand, he sat beside her and prayed out loud for a successful search and that Jeanette would be okay.

"Amen." Carol wasn't sure when the efforts to find Jeanette had become her personal mission, but her heart lightened a fraction at the reminder that the outcome of today's search was in God's hands. She nibbled on a piece of toast, but strained to swallow it. What if God didn't give them success? Then what?

"Let's just take it one step at a time," Harvey said as if reading her mind.

Carol struggled through half her breakfast, but finally stood and picked up her plate. "We should go. There's lots to do."

Carol dropped Harvey off at the police station with the map, then continued to Bread on Arrival. Laura and Molly were already hard at work, and the homey aroma of fresh baking spilled out into the street. Carol put on an apron and joined them, explaining that Harvey was planning to collaborate with Officer Drummond on mapping out search areas.

"Has anyone heard from Annemarie this morning?" Molly asked.

"No," Carol said. "I figured if she had news we hadn't heard, Bridget would phone us."

"Laura said Annemarie's dad stayed at the house last night." Molly brushed egg wash over a batch of bread loaves destined for the oven. "And it makes sense he would. But I couldn't help but remember Bridget's initial suspicions of him. Do you think we should be worried about ulterior motives?"

"I don't know what to think about him," Carol said. "He claims to have an alibi, but I haven't verified it. Hopefully the police have."

"Officer Drummond seems to be taking the case very seriously," Laura said. "I'm sure he has."

"Here's hoping," Carol muttered, then got to work on a batch of Selkirk bannocks, hoping the familiar task would soothe her frazzled nerves.

Harvey and Officer Drummond arrived at the bakery's back door about an hour later, and Carol let them in. Harvey held the corkboard, which now had many more pins stuck into it, and Officer Drummond was carrying a large easel.

"Where do you want to set this up?" Harvey asked as he entered. "In front of the fireplace?"

"Sure." Carol led the way to the front, where the men made quick work of setting up the easel. Hamish and Molly were handling the trickle of customers for the moment, so Carol examined the map. "Wow, there are a lot more places to look than I'd anticipated. I hope we have enough volunteers."

"We've only reached half of the known owners of green Saabs so far," Officer Drummond said, his face drawn and his eyes bloodshot. He must have worked through much of the night. "Hopefully Wilma can get hold of the remaining three this morning so we can eliminate a few more of these pins."

"That would still leave us with six fairly large areas," Carol observed. "It'll spread our volunteers pretty thin."

"I'm afraid it's the best we can do." The officer pointed to the largest area. "The chief has already dispatched our search and rescue team to comb this area. It's got a lot of difficult terrain, including numerous ravines, and I didn't want our volunteers getting injured. The team has a tracking dog too, so he should be able to sniff out if Jeanette tumbled down a ravine. And we'll have paramedics standing by."

"It sounds as if you thought of everything," Carol said appreciatively.

"It's not our first go-round," Drummond replied grimly.

Carol grimaced, reminded of a long-ago summer she'd visited the Upper Peninsula with her family. While they'd been there, a little boy had gone missing for two days. Firefighters had found the boy, but Carol's mother had hugged her tightly and made her promise never to wander off in the woods, clearly imagining what the alternative could have been.

Clearly sensing her unease, Harvey gave Carol a sideways hug. "We'll find her."

"I was hoping the Beamsville sheriff's office would've picked up our car thief by now," Officer Drummond went on. "He could help us focus on one area."

"Have you asked the cell phone company to try to ping Jeanette's phone?" Harvey asked.

"They tried, but couldn't get it," the officer said. "It's either out of battery, switched off, or out of range. The last ping they picked up from the phone was a little after nine a.m. Wednesday morning west of town, which is another reason I opted to concentrate the SAR team on that area. But we have Fergus and a few other volunteer firefighters to help with the remaining search areas, and I'll assign one officer to each location. With so much ground to cover, I'm afraid that's the best I can do."

Carol sent up a fervent prayer that the best would be good enough.

Volunteers began arriving a short while later, and Molly and Carol took charge of welcoming them while Laura and Hamish handled the bakehouse's day-to-day tasks.

Just before eight o'clock, Annemarie and her father entered and beelined toward Officer Drummond. "Any news since we last spoke?" Mr. Franklin asked without preamble.

"I'm afraid not." Drummond pointed to the map. "These are the areas where we're going to focus today's search. Did your wife favor any particular trail over another?"

Mr. Franklin frowned. "I never paid a lot of attention when she talked about where she walked." He raked his fingers through his hair and glanced toward the front counter. "Can I get a coffee?"

Carol bustled over to pour him one. "I'm surprised you came out this morning when we still had no firm sightings to go on. I thought you had a big meeting."

"I postponed it," he said, his voice gravelly as if he hadn't gotten enough sleep . . . or possibly none at all, given the dark circles under his eyes. "Finding my wife is more important."

Carol handed him his cup. "Of course." When he pulled out his wallet to pay, she held up her hand. "Coffee's on the house for all our volunteers."

He sighed. "Thank you. For everything."

Volunteers of all ages and walks of life soon packed the café area. Fergus mingled with other members of the Loch Mallaig Volunteer Fire Company near the front window, while a dozen or so college-age kids—likely Annemarie's friends—lingered around the fireplace. Even the Bakehouse Three's fellow Loch Mallaig shopkeepers had come, including Doreen from Thistle and That, Henry from The Artful Codger, Ewan Loganach from Two Scots Guesthouse B&B, and Cameron MacPhee from MacPhee's Family Drugstore.

When Carol had welcomed Henry, he'd mentioned that he'd closed his shop for the morning and put a sign in his window urging any shoppers who stopped by to join him in the search. Carol couldn't help but admire how he'd put the needs of a hurting member of the community ahead of his business interests. If Jeanette's husband had been half as willing to do so in the past, they might not be looking for her today.

Doreen studied the map. "Jeanette loves owls. When she visits my shop, she's always admiring anything depicting an owl in some form or another."

Carol nodded, remembering the numerous owl artifacts adorning the Franklins' home.

Doreen pointed to a spot on the map that didn't have a pin. "I heard there have been sightings of the snowy owl here. I think it's definitely something she would've been keen to see, so it would be a good idea to search that area for her."

"Indeed," Henry spoke up. "She does love owls. She admired an owl ornament in my shop as well. A fine idea, Ms. Giobsan."

Doreen broke into a surprised smile and nodded her appreciation for his support.

Jane Thomson pointed to another area on the map with one of the knitting needles she'd been working with while waiting for everyone to arrive. "I picnicked at this park with my grandchildren Wednesday morning. There were no other cars in the parking lot or dog walkers in the area."

Officer Drummond removed the pin from the map.

Henry gestured toward a location about fifteen miles northwest of town. "I stopped at this trailhead for a stroll about ten o'clock Wednesday morning. I was out making a delivery and was a little early, so I stretched my legs to kill some time. There were no other cars there then."

"Jeanette was last seen leaving our house shortly after nine. If she drove directly to the trailhead, she would've arrived long before ten," Mr. Franklin said.

Officer Drummond clasped the pin, but seemed to take a moment to consider whether to pull it. "The problem is we don't know if she stopped anywhere else first."

"Except that no one else has reported seeing her after nine o'clock," Molly pointed out.

"Right." Drummond yanked the pin and moved it to the snowy owl location.

Once they were fairly certain the bulk of their volunteer force had arrived, Carol divided them into groups of about twelve and assigned each one to a search area.

Carol and Harvey teamed up to operate a command post at one of the trailhead areas to monitor that groups' findings. As Carol followed the volunteers streaming out the door to travel to their assigned areas, she overheard Mr. Franklin ask another searcher if they could switch assignments.

The woman agreed, thereby rerouting Mr. Franklin to the parking lot adjacent to the national forest north of town that provided access to a couple of well-groomed trails, as well as several rugged ones.

Now, why would he favor that particular location over the one I gave him? Carol didn't like the answers that bombarded her thoughts. With grim reserve, she pulled aside the north group's leader and traded spots. She'd feel better if she could personally supervise the command post at Mr. Franklin's new location . . . just in case.

9

An hour later, Carol's spirits lifted at the excitement in the voice of the volunteer on the other end of her cell phone.

"We're about fifty yards west of the path." The volunteer's voice faded for a moment while someone else spoke in the background. "It's where the trail makes a sharp turn east."

Carol leaned over the picnic table that held her command station supplies and studied the forest map the police had given her. "Okay, I found it. Not far from the lake?"

The faint sound of the volunteer consulting his partner came through the phone. "We're not sure. We can't see the lake from where we are. But I think there's a way for me to get the GPS coordinates from my phone."

"Don't worry about that right now," Carol said. "What did you find?"

"A crumpled bakery bag. Jeanette's daughter said her mom always carries oatcakes from your bakery when she hikes, right?"

Carol's spirits nosedived. "She does. You were smart to call it in." Carol strained to keep her voice bright and encouraging. "But I'm afraid we always package her order in a box. Keep looking though. That's the kind of detail that might lead us to her."

No sooner had that volunteer disconnected than another searcher came racing from the woods carrying a muddy ball cap. She stopped a few yards from Carol and hunched over, her hands on her knees, trying to catch her breath.

"What did you find?" Carol eyed the Great Lake Loons ball cap speculatively. It appeared as if it had been out in the elements for a lot longer than a couple of days.

The young woman straightened and handed Carol the hat. "We spotted this snagged in some bushes part of the way down a really steep drop next to the trail. There were a lot of paw prints around too. We were thinking if the dog bolted after a squirrel or something, he could've yanked her over the edge."

Carol grimaced at the cap, which couldn't possibly fit a child much older than five or six, let alone an adult.

The young woman swallowed a long pull from her water bottle. The temperature was already in the upper 80s and it wasn't even ten o'clock yet. Carol hated to think how it would affect their older searchers.

"My partner is working his way down the ravine to see if he can spot her," the volunteer went on as she refilled her bottle from a large jug a local water supply company had donated.

Carol bit her lip, hating to douse her enthusiasm. "Good work," she said, hoping the brightness in her voice didn't sound as fake to the woman as it felt to Carol. "I'm afraid this is likely a child's cap." She demonstrated its size by holding it over her head. "But this is exactly the kind of evidence that could show us her trail, so keep up the good work."

The young woman visibly deflated. "I was so excited to find it that I didn't even register how small it is. I'd better go see how Erik's doing." She took off at a slower jog than the sprint that had brought her to Carol.

Halfway through the morning, Carol checked in with each of the other command post leaders. They'd had similar finds but nothing to lead them to Jeanette or even convince them they'd found the area where she'd hiked Wednesday morning.

At half past eleven, Bread on Arrival's hearse parked along the road near Carol's command post. Hamish climbed out and hauled a folding table from the back. "Laura sent me with scones and cookies for our volunteers. She was going to make sandwiches but feared they'd spoil in the heat." He set the table up beside the water dispenser and tromped back to the hearse. A moment later he returned with two large bakery boxes. "Will this be enough for your group?"

Carol peeked in the top box and did a quick count. "Should be. Thanks."

Hamish pulled a white handkerchief from his back pocket and wiped his brow. "Och, it sure is a hot one."

"Have you heard how the searchers at the other areas are holding up?"

"Aye. More than a few of the seniors were packing it in."

Carol sighed. She couldn't blame them. The heat was zapping her energy and she wasn't even moving, let alone walking up and down hills on uneven terrain.

Hamish replaced the handkerchief. "But Bridget's neighbor has rounded up some high school students who have promised to come after their job finishes for the day. They're working at a kids' summer camp that lets out at half past two."

"Fresh eyes will be very welcome by then, I think."

Hamish nodded in agreement. "I'd best be going. Still have two more stops to make. Keep up the good work." Hamish's positivity rang hollow to Carol. She would have preferred his usual surly attitude to this put-on cheer.

Shortly past noon, Harvey ambled toward the command post with Jack Franklin. Carol had asked her husband to partner with him to keep an eye on him for her. Harvey had a gift for reading people, especially those fond of bending the truth.

"Any chance these are for us?" Harvey jutted his chin toward the bakery boxes.

"They sure are," Carol said. "Help yourself."

Harvey held the box open for Mr. Franklin but, swatting at a mosquito on his arm, the businessman shook his head and fixed his attention on Carol. "I thought searching the area closest to where Jeanette's car was found would be best, but I'm afraid I don't see my contribution to the search effort being of much help at this point," he said, a touch of exasperation in his tone. "I'm going to head into the office and get my meeting out of the way so I can be fully available to my wife and daughter when Jeanette is found."

"I can understand that," Carol said, feeling slightly sheepish that she'd suspected his motives for switching search areas. He'd merely been thinking logically.

He handed her his business card. "Please contact me immediately if there are any new developments. I want to be there when they find her."

"Of course."

Harvey waited until the man had walked to his car, then sidled over to Carol with his scone and cup of water. "He didn't do anything suspicious that I could see," he reported. "Didn't talk much either. He's a bit of a pokey walker. I get the sense he's not much of an outdoors type. Or maybe he was just having trouble getting around in those new hiking boots. The mosquitoes were no picnic either. Or I should say they were making a picnic out of us."

Carol offered an empathetic smile, thankful the nasty insects preferred the woods to the sunny clearing where she'd set up. "Did you spot any signs Jeanette might have walked the trail the two of you tracked?"

Harvey finished chewing his bite of scone before replying. "There were plenty of paw prints in the muddy sections on the trails. Hard to say if any belonged to a springer spaniel." He tugged off his cap and wiped his sweaty brow. "We did run into a hiker with a dog I estimated to be about the same size as a springer, and the muddy paw print it left on Jack's pant leg was similar to several prints we saw." Harvey chuckled. "I think that encounter was what made Jack call it a day. The man sure isn't crazy about dogs."

"Yet apparently Jeanette's dog adored him." *And his car.*

A white van slipped into the spot Mr. Franklin's BMW had vacated. A group of teen boys tumbled out of the back and a man Carol recognized climbed out of the driver's seat. Her gaze jerked to the logo on the side of the truck—Gambel's Heating and Air. *Steve's company.* The small sheltie yipping at the driver's heels confirmed his identity.

Carol felt a frisson of nerves, then tamped them down by reminding herself that only Molly had talked to Jeanette's would-be suitor at the dog park Wednesday night, so chances were good he wouldn't know her.

"We're here to help search for the missing woman," Steve announced as he reached Carol at the picnic table that held her makeshift command station. "Officer Drummond said you might be able to use a few more volunteers here."

"Yes. Thank you." Carol smiled at the teens now lined up in front of her eyeing the bakery boxes. "You boys can help yourselves to a couple of cookies before you start, if you like." She knew from her years of teaching adolescents to specify a number so they didn't wipe out the whole box.

Steve must have learned the same thing, because he added, "That's two each, guys. Leave the rest for the other volunteers."

Harvey's eyes twinkled with amusement as he held the box open for them.

Carol returned her attention to Steve. He hadn't identified Jeanette by name. Did he not realize the missing woman was the same person he'd been corresponding with through Puppy Love? Granted, they'd only exchanged first names, so why would he?

Unless he'd somehow orchestrated her disappearance to disrupt Mr. Franklin's business negotiations.

"Do you know the missing woman?" Carol asked, trying not to reveal her suspicions.

Steve shook his head. "I volunteer at the youth center and got a call from the director that some of the boys wanted to help search. He asked me to supervise them."

"It's very kind of you to take time off work to do that."

"When you're the boss, it's a little easier." Steve studied the forest map Carol had splayed out on the table. "Where do you want us to start?"

The area had five official trails. Two were designated cross use for hikers and bikers, one allowed horse access, and the other two were reserved for hikers alone. Carol pointed to an extra loop at the far end of the horse trail. "No one has been out this far yet."

Steve traced his finger along the trail to a creek, then followed the creek to where it met the road a few miles south of their present location. "I'll drive the boys to this point and we can cut in to the trail by going along the creek. It will save a lot of time."

"That's a good plan."

Steve clapped his hands. "Okay boys, back in the van. We're going to park down the road."

Carol handed him a Bread on Arrival card with her cell number written on the back. "If you find anything, phone me at this number."

He grinned at the shortbread cookie logo on the front of the card. "Cute. I've seen your delivery hearse around town, but I haven't had the chance to drop in yet."

"You're welcome any time."

He scooped up a shortbread cookie and sampled a bite. "Yum. I'll definitely have to drop by."

Carol watched Steve, Jinx, and the boys pile back in the van, chewing at her lip all the while.

"What's wrong?" Harvey asked.

"That was the guy who's been corresponding with Jeanette Franklin on the dating site," she said.

"And you're not sure you can trust him."

"Right."

Harvey gently squeezed her shoulder. "I doubt he'll get up to any monkey business with four young scrappers along as witnesses."

"That's true. And he didn't balk at the assignment. I thought he might push back if he had a specific area he wanted to ensure no one else searched."

"If he'd been hoping to do that, he would've shown up first thing this morning."

"Unless he really didn't hear about the search until recently." Carol pulled up a satellite map of the area on her phone and zoomed in on the creek Steve intended to follow. The trees were so thick that much of the creek was barely visible.

Harvey broke into her thoughts. "It makes sense for him to cut across country instead of taking the trail all the way from here. Don't read more into it than there is."

"You're right. I was actually wondering if there might be more places like that, where a hiker might park far away from the trailhead and cut through the woods to pick up a trail." Carol studied the paper map once more. "We sent the searchers out to look for signs Jeanette had been on a given trail or signs of someone veering off it, but what if she never made it to the trail from where she parked?" She huffed a frustrated breath. "If only the Beamsville sheriff would find the car thief already."

"If only," Harvey repeated with another supportive shoulder squeeze.

Carol's phone rang, making her jump. She glanced at the screen but didn't recognize the number. "This might be one of our volunteers." She hit connect. "Hello?"

"We've found a women's sneaker, blue, size 8," the male voice on the other end of the line said.

"Where?" Carol asked.

"A stone's throw from the south end of the gold bike path." The volunteer recited GPS coordinates. "Should I pick it up or leave it for the police?"

Carol's heart raced. "Don't touch it for now. I'll ask the officer in charge and call you back." Carol started to tap in Drummond's number, then decided to call Annemarie first.

The girl picked up on the first ring.

"What size shoe does your mom wear?"

"Size 7, just like me."

"Never an 8? One of my volunteers found a size 8 women's sneaker."

"Mom always wore hiking boots for walking in the woods. She said she needed the ankle support."

"Of course." Carol smacked her forehead. She'd known that. "That's all I needed. Thanks."

Carol called her volunteer back and told him the shoe wasn't Jeanette's, then suffered through the rest of the afternoon. The hours dragged on, punctuated by similar brief spurts of hope. By midafternoon, most of the volunteers under Carol's charge had trickled away, and by four o'clock, the water supply company had retrieved their water jug and Hamish had been back to collect his table.

Carol studied her list of volunteers. She'd heard nothing from Steve, but she'd checked off all the rest as having left for the day. "So whose gray Pontiac is that parked at the edge of the lot?" Carol asked Harvey.

"No clue. Were there any latecomers who didn't make your list?"

"I don't even remember that car arriving."

"Could be a blueberry picker," Harvey suggested. "Jack and I happened on one really nice patch in a sunny clearing this morning. I couldn't resist stopping and sampling a few."

"The blueberry doesn't fall far from the bush," Carol said, thinking of their grandkids' love of berry picking—and eating.

Carol packed her map and any other remaining supplies into their car, then paused to assess the Pontiac. She noticed a faint trail leading from the gray car across the grassy ditch and into the woods.

"Since I didn't get Steve's number from him, I thought we could drive down to where he said he'd park to check on his status," she told Harvey as he climbed into the driver's seat. "But I hate to leave if we still have a searcher out there."

"Let's go see Steve, then we can double back to check if this car is still here."

Carol got into the car, then peered out the passenger window as Harvey started the engine. Still no sign of the Pontiac's owner. Her phone rang with another unfamiliar number. "Hello?"

"This is Steve Gambel. I just wanted to let you know I'm taking the boys home now. We didn't find anything aside from a few crushed soda cans and old water bottles—nothing that looked as if it would've been discarded in the last couple of days."

"Thanks for checking in, and for coming to help," Carol said.

"No problem," Steve replied. "I'm just proud of my boys for wanting to take part. And I sure hope somebody else has better luck than we did."

"Same here," Carol said, then wished Steve a good night and disconnected the call.

"Looks like we have our answer about the Pontiac driver too." Harvey nodded toward the rearview mirror.

Carol twisted in her seat to peer through the rear window. A white-haired woman with a hunched back set two blueberry-laden baskets on the hood of the gray car, then fished through the fanny pack at her waist until she found her car key and unlocked the door.

"I suddenly have a craving for your blueberry streusel muffins," Harvey said. "Do you think we have time to pick a few cups of berries before we leave?"

Carol shrugged. "It shouldn't take us long. And it'll give me time to think about our next move."

That was all the permission Harvey needed. He grabbed an empty bakery box from the back seat and bounced out of the car before Carol had her seat belt unbuckled. By the time she joined him on the side of the road, he'd already grilled the blueberry picker on the best place to go.

Harvey pointed beyond the faint trail Carol had noticed leading away from the Pontiac. "She says there's a clearing not far past these trees where the picking is good. Let's go."

The good news was that they had no trouble finding the berry-laden bushes right where the woman had told them they'd be. The bad news was that, despite almost half an hour of brainstorming while they picked, at the end, Carol wasn't any closer to fresh ideas for finding Jeanette.

Harvey's phone rang, and his eyebrows went up in surprise when he checked the screen. "Why is the bakery calling me?"

Carol snagged the phone from his hand. "Hello?"

"Carol, where are you?" Molly blurted. "We've been trying to reach you for the past half hour."

"I'm sorry, I must have left my phone in the car," Carol said, then recognized the urgency in Molly's tone. "Did they find Jeanette?"

"No, but they found the car thief," Molly said. "Officer Drummond is heading over to the Franklins' at five to fill them in on what he's learned. Bridget called to say Annemarie would like us all to be there."

Carol locked eyes with Harvey. "We'll drive straight there."

By the time they arrived, the Franklins' driveway was full of cars, including Laura's, Molly's, Bridget's, Annemarie's, and her father's. "At least we got here before Officer Drummond," Carol said to Harvey.

Annemarie invited them into the great room, where everyone else had congregated. She appeared much more hopeful than she had twenty-four hours earlier, despite the day's unproductive ground search. "I was a mess an hour ago," she confessed to Carol while they waited for Officer Drummond. "For all the litter, odd shoes, and scraps of cloth the searchers found, not a single item looked like anything of Mom's."

"I know, it's so frustrating," Carol said.

"And it's been two and a half days now." Annemarie toyed with the fringe rimming a throw pillow sitting on the couch beside her. "With how out of whack her blood sugar gets sometimes, I'm so worried about how sick she could be if she's not eating. And if she is eating, there could be problems with how her body is reacting to it without her medication."

Carol nodded her understanding. Given how much ground the searchers had covered that day without finding a single scrap of evidence, she was beginning to wonder if the assumption that Jeanette had lost her way while out for a hike had been wrong.

That means the possibility is still on the table that someone harmed Jeanette. Someone like Mr. Franklin or Steve Gambel or a crazed car thief, Carol thought grimly. Hopefully whatever Drummond had learned from the Beamsville sheriff's department would shed light on the situation.

A sharp rap at the door made them all jump. Mr. Franklin let Officer Drummond in and escorted him to the great room.

"I'll get right to the point," the policeman said. "Sheriff Bugle called to let me know they found the felon who stole Jeanette's car."

"That's wonderful news," Carol said. Then she noticed the deep furrow in Drummond's brow, which suggested that what he'd learned about the car thief might not be good news for their search.

"His name's Cedric Button," Officer Drummond continued. "Unfortunately, it appears someone else beat the deputies to him."

Mr. Franklin crossed his arms and shot the officer a hostile frown. "What do you mean beat them to him?"

Drummond gazed back solemnly. "They found Button facedown in a field. Dead."

10

"Someone killed the car thief?" Carol asked, disbelief coloring her voice. It made no sense. Who would hunt down Jeanette's car thief? Surely not Jeanette.

Annemarie sucked in a ragged breath and turned so pale it appeared she might faint. Her father coaxed her into a chair.

"Possibly," Officer Drummond said in response to Carol's question. "Cedric's body was found not far from where the car had been abandoned. And the shoe prints at the scene suggest he ran into the field from the car with one, maybe two others."

"But how did he die?" Laura asked.

"A blunt force injury to the side of the head. But it's still unclear if the injury was the result of the crash or if someone struck him."

"Why would someone strike him?" Molly asked.

"We have no idea," Drummond answered. "A case of road rage maybe, but that's just speculation. Unfortunately, what his death means for our investigation is that we still have no idea where Jeanette's car was parked when Cedric hot-wired it. And since today's searches exhausted all the tips we've received—without turning up a single new clue—we've run out of places to look."

Annemarie shot to her feet. "We can't give up."

Her father folded her into his arms. "We won't, pumpkin. I'll hire a private investigator if I need to."

"What do you think?" Molly whispered to Laura and Carol.

Carol tugged them a little further out of earshot of father and daughter. "I think we need to look closer at who might have wanted to make Jeanette disappear."

"Agreed," Laura said.

As Carol listened to Officer Drummond promise the Franklins that his office would continue to follow up on every tip they got, she couldn't help but think there had to be something more proactive they could do to find Jeanette than wait for leads to come to them.

While Mr. Franklin walked Officer Drummond to the door, Carol gave Annemarie a hug. "We're going to go too. I have a few more questions I'd like to ask Officer Drummond before he leaves. But we're not giving up the search." She motioned to her friends and husband to join her, and they all hurried out after the police officer.

"I wish I'd had better news for you," Drummond admitted. "You did a fabulous job organizing the search, and it's a shame nothing came of it."

"What else are you doing to find Jeanette?" Carol asked. "Have you tried tracing her credit cards?"

The officer's eyebrow quirked, and if the situation weren't so dire, Carol suspected he would've made a sarcastic comment along the lines of "I wish I'd thought of that." However, he seemed to understand they just needed to know he hadn't left any stone unturned.

"Yes, I ran the credit cards," he said. "They haven't been used in the past three months. According to her daughter, she's been paying cash for everything since the separation."

"And you checked with all the hospitals?" Laura asked.

Drummond nodded. "Every last one within a hundred miles. I also questioned the harbormaster about the family boat," he volunteered, surprising Carol by being so forthcoming—perhaps their efforts in organizing the search had earned his trust. "It turns out the boat wasn't in its mooring Wednesday morning when he returned from his break at ten o'clock. It's back now, but he didn't see who sailed it in."

"Did you ask Mr. Franklin if he took it out?" Molly asked.

A wave of queasiness hit Carol as an image of the estranged husband pushing his wife overboard flashed through her mind.

"Franklin claims he was in meetings all day," Officer Drummond said. "Several people confirmed the alibi."

Harvey scratched at the late-day stubble on his chin. "Do you think Jeanette took the boat out?"

Drummond's expression became skeptical. "If she did, where'd she go afterward? No one has seen her since nine o'clock Wednesday morning, including the regulars at the harbor. Franklin says he's given a few friends permission to use the boat and suspects one of them had it out. He doubted Jeanette would take it on her own."

Carol bit her lip, thinking Jeanette may not have gone out in it alone, but whoever she'd been with could've returned alone. "Did you check the boat for signs of a struggle or foul play of some sort?"

"With Franklin's permission, yes." Drummond splayed his hands. "It was clean."

"So that's it?" Laura frowned. "Unless more tips come in, we're just supposed to sit back and hope Jeanette turns up?"

Drummond heaved a sigh. "I wish I had more to offer. But without any leads, there's not much more we can do." On that pessimistic note, the officer took his leave.

"I can't accept that just twiddling our thumbs is the only option," Laura said as she watched Officer Drummond drive away.

"Has anyone checked with the local dog kennels to see if Jeanette boarded her dog?" Molly asked. "Maybe she took a flight somewhere and her car was stolen from the airport's long-term parking lot."

Bridget, who must've slipped out of the house as Drummond

was leaving, piped up at Molly's question. "Annemarie checked with dog kennels and animal shelters. No one had seen any dog matching Scout's description. The shelters all said that if he's wearing a dog tag, they'd contact her as soon as he was brought in."

"Does he wear one?" Laura asked.

Bridget nodded. "He's got the town license tag, and Mrs. Franklin had her contact information etched on the back."

"The family's home number?" Carol clarified. "Or Jeanette's cell number?" *The number she wasn't answering.*

Bridget paled. "I don't know. I'll check with Annemarie."

"I'm sure the police have contacted the animal shelters too," Harvey said. "Officer Drummond seems to have covered every possible base." He nudged Carol toward the car. "It's been a long, hot day. You ladies need to rest too. Things will look brighter in the morning."

He was right of course. Carol practically melted into the passenger seat on the way home. She had scarcely slept the previous night, and being out in the heat all day had zapped any energy she'd mustered. It was a wonder she was still awake.

Her heart warmed as they drove into view of their cozy one-and-a-half-story log cabin. "I'm grateful you didn't insist on our home being as rustic as it looks," she mused to her husband.

"How do you mean?"

She picked at the sweaty top clinging to her skin. "I'm looking forward to a long shower and sleeping in air-conditioned comfort."

Harvey chuckled. "Not going to sit out and watch the sunset?"

Many nights she loved to slip out onto the porch and watch the sun sink over their chicken coop, but . . . "It's been quite a day. I just want shower, food, and bed, in that order."

"I'll put burgers on the grill for us while you get clean, how does that sound?"

"Perfect."

Carol tried to put the day's disappointments out of her mind as she stood under the cool stream of water, but the notion that she'd overlooked a glaring clue prickled at the back of her mind. She mentally reviewed the day but nothing stood out as significant. And yet, the uneasy feeling wouldn't relent.

Harvey called that supper was ready just as Carol was finishing getting dressed. She leaned down to pet Pascal's head, which was barely peeking out from under the bed. "Gotcha," she said. He lifted his head a tiny bit and lingered for a moment, just enough to get one more rub, then retreated into his sanctuary.

Harvey was picking up two dinner plates loaded with burgers, corn on the cob, and grilled vegetables when Carol stepped into the kitchen. "I thought we might eat in front of the evening news tonight," he said. "What do you think?"

"Sure. I'd like to see what they're reporting on the search for Jeanette if we're not too late." Carol followed him to the living room.

"They usually recap the top stories halfway through their broadcast." Harvey set down the plates on the coffee table and clicked the TV on.

They sat down to news that there was no break in sight for the heat wave.

Carol groaned. "I don't remember the summers being this hot when we were younger. But I guess I should be grateful I get to shift between baking, working the counter, and doing bookkeeping in an air-conditioned office. Laura rarely gets away from the heat of the ovens."

Carol's thoughts turned to Jeanette, possibly out in this unrelenting heat and humidity for nearing sixty hours. Surely if she were injured, her dog would've gone for help or attracted attention with his barking.

Her mind itched again with the feeling she'd ignored an important clue. Was it the fact that the dog had disappeared too?

Carol had limited experience with dog ownership. Were they so loyal they wouldn't leave a mistress's side if she were in distress? Not even to get help?

"This is it." Harvey grabbed the remote control and turned up the volume.

While footage of volunteers exploring the trails played in the background, a maternal newscaster with a blonde bob detailed the search efforts. Next, pictures of Jeanette and Scout filled the screen as the anchor entreated anyone who'd seen them to call the tip line.

As the images on screen disappeared and the broadcast moved on to another topic, Carol's corn cob fell to her plate with a thud.

Harvey glanced over. "Are you okay?"

Carol set her dinner aside. "Where is that stack of missing posters I had?"

"On the hall table, I think. What is it?"

"He's wearing a red tag." She hurried to the hall and grabbed one of the posters, then studied the picture of Scout. It was a photocopy, so the dog tag appeared black instead of red, but in the image on the news broadcast, it had definitely been red.

"Who?" Harvey asked, joining her. "What are you talking about?"

"Scout. In the picture, he's wearing a red dog tag. Just like the one Henry Roberts had in his pocket."

Harvey looked at the photo. "Red is the color of the Loch Mallaig dog license tags. Everyone with a dog should have one."

Carol frowned. Did Henry have a dog? He'd never mentioned one. Carol dug through her purse. "Have you seen my cell phone?"

"I put it on the charger."

Carol unplugged it from the cable and called Molly. "Do you know if Henry Roberts owns a dog?" Molly had been to Henry's store at least twice, and as a dog owner herself, she might've talked to him about pets.

"I don't know," Molly answered. "Not that he mentioned. Why?"

"Don't you remember? He pulled a red dog tag out of his pocket the other day when he was making change for us."

"Every dog has one of those, even Angus."

"Sure, but Henry had it in his pocket and we're not sure he even has a dog."

"Okay . . ." The hesitation and inflection in Molly's voice made it clear that she wasn't making the connection.

"What if the dog tag is Scout's?"

Silence hung between them for a long moment.

Finally Molly spoke. "You think Henry Roberts has Scout and Jeanette? But what possible motive could he have?"

Carol deflated. "I have no idea. But I've had this feeling we were missing something, and now I'm sure that the tag is what it was."

"But he didn't act nervous or try to hide the tag when it spilled onto the counter with his change. If he were up to something criminal and the dog tag had the potential to give him away, don't you think it would have affected his behavior?"

Carol's brain acknowledged that what Molly was saying made sense, but as she stared at the image of the dog tag dangling from Scout's collar, she couldn't bring herself to let the idea go just yet. "Maybe Doreen knows if he has a dog. I'll try calling her." Doreen seemed to be making it her mission to learn everything there was to know about the man, going as far as to wonder if his business was shady—surely she'd know if he had a dog.

When Carol disconnected, the look Harvey gave her was as skeptical as Molly's voice had been. "It's significant," she insisted. "It's got to be."

Just when Carol thought her next call would go to Doreen's voice mail, the shop owner picked up. "Does Henry Roberts have a dog?" Carol blurted, bypassing pleasantries.

"Why?" Doreen asked. After receiving an explanation, she said, "I don't know, but I can find out. I'll get back to you." She hung up before Carol could thank her.

Carol stared at the phone, then shifted her gaze to Harvey. "Should I call Officer Drummond and share my suspicions of Henry Roberts or wait until Doreen finds out if he has a dog of his own that the tag might belong to?"

"I say wait." Harvey's tone was decisive.

Carol wavered, her emotions playing tug-of-war inside her chest. "But time could be running out. Can Jeanette wait?"

11

All night, Carol dreamed about dogs of all breeds jumping and frolicking around her, their red tags bouncing out of view every time she tried to read one. If it hadn't been for the dreams, she would've said she hadn't slept. She sure felt like she hadn't.

Unable to go back to sleep after her latest distressing dream, Carol stared up at the bedroom ceiling. "You awake?" she whispered.

No answer came from Harvey.

She rolled on to her side and discovered his side of the bed was already empty. Her gaze shifted to the bureau where he'd set out his fishing clothes the night before. They were gone. She flung off the covers and jumped out of bed. Pulling up the blinds, she blinked at the brightness of the rising sun. "I guess I did sleep. And I'm late for work."

As she dashed to the bathroom, the aroma of brewing coffee filled her with appreciation for her thoughtful Harvey. She dressed in record time, poured the coffee he'd left for her into a travel mug, and grabbed her keys and purse. Only then did she remember she still had to feed her hens.

She quickly stashed her purse and coffee in the car along with the box of blueberries she and Harvey had picked the day before—she planned to mix them into the muffins he'd requested—but she slowed her pace as she neared the chicken coop. Her chickens were sensitive to being startled, and she didn't want to disturb their laying. She opened the escape hatch to their run, and the sight of them racing out to greet her soothed her frazzled nerves. She spoke brightly to her girls as she threw out some fresh grain for them. Next she checked their laying box—one egg from each, despite this brutal heat. "Yeh bonnie lasses are *braw*," she called out to them as she latched the henhouse door. She was convinced they were happier when she cooed at them with a Scottish lilt.

A few minutes later, with eggs put away in the house, she climbed into her car and glanced at the dashboard clock. She blew out a disgusted huff. No matter how many times she tried to beat Laura in to get an early start on the day's baking, she rarely seemed to succeed.

And it wasn't as if Laura was used to a bakery's schedule. The high-pressure chef job she'd left in NYC had been at chic nighttime hot spot 29 North. The hours had been a real relationship killer, not that Laura had dated anyone seriously since a broken engagement more than twenty years earlier. Then again, needing to go to bed early enough so she could start work with the sun wasn't going to help her fare much better here.

Thistle and That was still dark next door when Carol drove down Tattie Bogle Road and slowed for her turn into the Bread on Arrival lot. Not that she'd expected to see Doreen this early. Part of her had hoped to, however, because waiting until Doreen stopped in for her morning bakery fix to find out Henry Roberts's dog ownership status was going to feel like forever.

Doreen might have been nowhere to be found, but someone else was out earlier than expected. Bridget's dark blue Honda Civic was already in the lot when Carol parked, and the girl was just disappearing through the bakery's back door.

Carol hurried after her, wondering why Bridget was at the bakehouse hours before her shift was supposed to start. "Do you have news?" she asked as she entered the kitchen.

An anxious Bridget bobbed her head. "Yes."

The sound of Angus clomping down the stairs—and of Molly scolding him for sneaking past her—interrupted Bridget before she could explain. Angus scampered into the kitchen but obediently stopped short just inside the doorway and pranced in a circle to get their attention. A moment later, Molly appeared. "You're going back upstairs before the shop opens," she warned him, then grinned at his antics.

"You're just in time to hear Bridget's news." Laura slipped a tray of bagels into the oven and set the timer. "Okay, Bridget, go ahead."

"Mr. Franklin has hired a private investigator," Bridget announced.

"That's good to hear." Molly poured herself a cup of coffee. "I feel better with a professional involved."

"I think you three are doing just as well as some old PI," Bridget said with a shrug, then got to the meat of her information. "Anyway, get this: Yesterday afternoon, Mr. Franklin settled on all the conditions for the sale of his company to that big conglomerate. But it'll only go into effect if they find Jeanette in time."

"What do you mean?" Carol frowned as she donned an apron and prepared to get to work while they discussed the case. That day's scones weren't going to bake themselves.

"The Franklins' company is incorporated, and Mr. Franklin and his wife hold the only shares, fifty-fifty. The deal can't go through without her signature."

"Or without a death certificate," Laura added somberly.

Carol shuddered. "That explains why he prioritized searching for his wife over the meeting yesterday morning."

"Do you really think he's that greedy?" Molly asked. "Fergus says he's doing this to prove his love to his wife."

"It certainly does make it seem less likely he had anything to do with her disappearance," Carol said.

"It makes our earlier theory about his competition kidnapping her more plausible though." Molly sipped her coffee. "Maybe we need to look into a new AC unit for the bakery." She raised an eyebrow. "If you get my drift."

"I'm sure the PI will scrutinize Mr. Franklin's competition," Carol said. "But I'd still like to pay Henry Roberts a visit and get another look at that dog tag he had. I'll go over later, after we get the day's baking in hand."

Bridget left with a promise to return for her shift, and Laura and Carol resumed baking while Molly handled the front of house's opening tasks.

Molly reentered the kitchen shortly before opening time with the slate from The Artful Codger in her hand. "What should today's special be?"

"I was thinking blueberry goodies for blue hair," Laura replied. "We really don't have enough blueberries to give much away for free, but I figure hardly anyone will try to claim it."

Molly chuckled. "Blueberry muffins for free? Don't be so sure. I bet Helga Hofmeister will try to pass off her dark gray hair as blue just to cash in."

Carol squirmed. "Maybe it's time we come up with a different kind of promotion. Officer Drummond accused us of folliclism."

Laura waved a dish towel at Carol. "He was teasing."

"Maybe, but you don't want to upset customers," Carol countered. "I'm sure some of them kind of resent they can't get something for free just because they don't have the hair color of the day."

Laura sighed. "Okay, we can retire the hair specials and think of something else."

"Why not write a trivia question about Loch Mallaig on your wee board every morning?" Hamish suggested as he entered the kitchen, pocketing his keys to the bakehouse. "Correct answers earn a discount."

Laura laughed. "Now why didn't I think of that?" She grinned at Hamish. "You're handy to have around, Hamish."

His cheeks pinked behind his white facial hair. "Och, now . . ." He cleared his throat. "Where shall I begin?"

Carol glanced at the clock. It was still early, but she didn't want to wait much longer for an answer to her question about the dog tag in Henry Roberts's pocket. "You can stock the trays for the display cases. I'm going to sneak over to The Artful Codger to see Henry about that dog tag. And I can ask him myself if he has a dog since I haven't heard back from Doreen."

"Doreen's gone," Hamish said as he washed his hands at the sink.

Carol frowned. "What do you mean gone?"

"I passed Wilma Guthrie on the sidewalk this morning," Hamish explained. "She said Doreen decided to take an impromptu vacation, doesn't know when she'll be back."

Carol stared at him, stunned. "I just talked to her last night. She didn't mention a thing about going away."

Molly's brow creased in alarm. "Did Wilma actually talk to Doreen?"

Hamish shrugged. "When isn't Wilma talking? But I don't know. She heard it from Doreen's part-timer."

Molly turned to Carol. "If she started snooping around Henry and he actually did have something to do with Jeanette's disappearance, maybe he figured . . ."

"What's one more disappearance?" Carol finished.

Laura burst into laughter. "Are you hearing yourselves? What possible motive could he have for hurting Jeanette or kidnapping her or whatever? Not to mention he's got to be pushing seventy, so unless he has an antique gun among his other treasures, I'm pretty sure either woman could escape him if she had to."

"I don't know." Molly quirked an eyebrow. "He may have a little snow up top, but he doesn't seem to have any trouble handling his own deliveries."

Laura shook her head. "He even closed his store yesterday to join in the search."

Molly's eyes widened. "But isn't it interesting that he convinced Officer Drummond to cross one of the search areas off the map?"

"He wasn't the only one to offer advice on which areas to search or not," Laura countered. "Or the first. Doreen was."

"Doreen, who is also now missing," Molly mused.

"She's on vacation!" Exasperation seeped through Laura's tone.

"Or that's what someone would like us to believe," Carol said, feeling as skeptical as Molly about the whole scenario. After all, Doreen never missed a day of work during prime tourist season. She'd said so herself. So why would she abandon ship when her store was struggling and she needed the sales more than ever?

"There's only one way to settle this." Carol untied her apron. "I'm going to see Henry Roberts right now."

Carol marched to The Artful Codger before she lost her nerve. Any concern she had that he wouldn't be there vanished at the sight of his delivery truck turning down the alley beside his shop.

By the time she reached the rear of his building, Henry was wheeling an armoire off the truck and onto his loading dock via a wooden ramp. "Morning," she called up to him.

He startled, then spun toward her. "Mrs. MacCallan. You surprised me."

"I'm sorry," she said. "But I needed to ask you something. And it's rather important."

Henry settled the dolly holding the armoire, then reached up and pulled a rope to close the truck's back door. "What is it?"

"Do you have a dog?"

"That's what you need to know?" He paused with his hand hovering above the dolly handle, his brow furrowed in confusion. "No, I don't have any pets. Although I was thinking a cat might come in useful to keep mice out of my storage bay."

While he wheeled the armoire into the warehouse, he expounded on the nests he'd been finding in everything from drawers to a pair of old boots. Carol squinted up at him, wondering if nerves had prompted him to give a three-minute answer to a yes-or-no question, or if he was just a natural conversationalist.

He climbed down the steps from the loading bay, putting them eye to eye. "Why do you ask?"

She forced an innocent smile. "I was just remembering the dog tag you had in your pocket the other day."

He appeared taken aback, but only for a moment. "Ah yes. I found that out on the sidewalk."

"Do you still have it? I'd like to see it."

"I should. Follow me." He led her around to the store's front door and used one of the keys dangling from a collection on his hip to open the lock.

She hesitated at the threshold, thinking about Doreen. What could've happened to her if she'd questioned the man as Carol was doing now? With a slight shake of the head, Carol talked sense into herself. When would Doreen have had the chance to question Henry? He only just got here, and it had been after closing time when Carol had called Doreen last night.

"Coming?" Henry was already halfway to his sales counter.

Buck up, Carol MacCallan, she told herself, then hurried inside. She reached the register just as the shop owner was reaching under the counter. He revealed a catchall dish, which he quickly started picking through. A moment later, he plucked the dog tag from the dish, squinted at it, then put on his reading glasses and recited the tag number. "Do you know whose dog it belongs to? I meant to call the town to find out, but it slipped my mind."

"May I see it?" Carol asked.

He handed it over without hesitation.

She flipped it over and gasped. *Scout* was etched at the top, followed by two phone numbers beneath it—Jeanette's cell number, and another one she guessed was the Franklins' landline.

Henry's face paled. "Do you think it belonged to Mrs. Franklin's dog? I should've looked more closely at the tag as soon as I picked it up."

Carol fixed a laser gaze on the man. "Exactly when and where did you find this tag?"

"Like I said before, I found it out on the sidewalk. I think it was Tuesday." His eyes shifted skyward as if he were searching his memory. "Yes, that's right. But Mrs. Franklin hadn't been to my shop since the week before. Her dog could have lost it then, or perhaps as they were passing by."

Carol wasn't ready to accept his claim at face value. Finding the tag the day *before* Jeanette's disappearance was far too convenient, not to mention unlikely, considering that was two days before he pulled it out of his pocket in front of her in his search for change. She didn't know about other men, but her husband emptied his pockets each night before removing his trousers. "What do you do with the change in your pockets at the end of the day?"

"I put it in a dish on my bedroom bureau."

"And the next morning? Do you return it to the pockets of whatever you're wearing?"

"Usually, yes," Henry answered. "I particularly remember putting the dog tag back into my pocket and telling myself I should leave it here in case one of my customers came searching for it."

Carol took a deep breath. She wanted to believe him. She really did. Like Laura had said, he seemed like a very nice man, and she hated being suspicious of anyone. But he'd learned of Jeanette and her dog going missing on Wednesday. Shouldn't that have prompted his curiosity about whose dog tag he'd found?

Carol held up the tag. "I'd better take this to the police."

"Go right ahead," Henry said. "Though I'm not sure what they might learn from it."

With a sigh, Carol shrugged. To be honest, she didn't know either—but she couldn't shake the possibility that it would lead the search for Jeanette right back to Henry's shop.

12

Carol handed Officer Drummond Scout's dog tag as she related her misgivings.

"Do you have any reason not to believe Mr. Roberts's explanation for how he came to possess it?" Drummond asked.

"I find it difficult to believe he'd empty it from his pockets two nights in a row without acting on it, especially when he'd heard about a missing woman and her dog the day after he found it."

The policeman bobbed his head in acknowledgment. "But Roberts has no discernible motive for harming or hiding Mrs. Franklin."

Carol rubbed her fingers against her throbbing temple. "True. But I couldn't get the incongruity out of my mind. It's got to be significant. We only have his word for it that he found the tag the day before she disappeared."

"But you can't think of any reason why he would want her to disappear."

Carol expelled a frustrated breath. "No I can't. Still, I thought you should know."

"I appreciate it." Drummond escorted her back to the police station lobby. "I'll pay him a visit. You take care."

By the time Carol returned to the bakehouse, it was bustling with customers. Molly and Hamish seemed to have everything out front well in hand, so Carol opted to focus on resupplying the blueberry streusel muffins. Baking usually relaxed her, and with any luck it would also ease the tension fueling her headache.

"You're back," Laura said, returning from the storage room as Carol was measuring out ingredients. "I was getting ready to regroup the search party. What did you learn?"

"The dog tag is Scout's, but Henry claims he found it outside his shop on Tuesday—before Jeanette and Scout disappeared. Officer Drummond seems to believe him."

Laura arched an auburn eyebrow. "Do you?"

Carol clenched her fist at the resurgence of the pounding in her head, then willed herself to relax. "I don't know. I hate not knowing whether she's alive or dead. What if we ignore a clue that could save her?"

"You didn't ignore it. You reported it to the police."

Carol dumped a cup of sugar into her baking bowl. "For all the good it did."

"You never know. Maybe Drummond will tail Roberts when he leaves the shop to see where he goes."

"You think so?" Carol dumped another cup of sugar into the bowl. "Was that my second cup or third?"

"Second."

"Right. I'd better focus on the recipe now." Carol sighed. "No need to add baking disasters to our existing chaos."

Forty minutes later, as Carol drew four dozen perfectly golden blueberry muffins from the oven, she realized her headache was gone. Baking had worked its magic once again, and this morning, she'd certainly needed it to free her mind of its fretting. Her heart panged to think how much worse the anguish must be for Annemarie and her father.

Carol set aside a few muffins for Harvey, then took the rest to the front counter. She glanced out the window and her breath caught. Hamish stood in front of the shop talking to Doreen's brother, Glenn, a stocky, dark-haired man dressed in a suit even though it was Saturday.

"Can you arrange these?" Carol asked Molly, then hurried to the door to catch the man before he left.

But Glenn Giobsan was coming, not going, and he tugged the door open at the same moment Carol's hand landed on the knob.

"Mr. Giobsan," Carol said, catching herself before she stumbled through the doorway.

He chuckled. "Please, Mr. Giobsan is my father. Call me Glenn. Carol, isn't it?"

"Yes." She stepped back to let him inside.

"Just who I wanted to see. Hamish said you talked to my sister last night. I was hoping you might be able to tell me where she's flitted off to."

"Actually, I was going to ask you the same thing. She said she'd have some information for me this morning, but it appears she's suddenly gone on vacation."

Glenn grunted. "I don't believe it for a second." He held up his phone. "She's not answering my calls." He turned on his heel, likely dissatisfied that Carol didn't have the information he was seeking.

"Wait," Carol called after him as he pushed open the door. "Do you think she could've been kidnapped or something?"

Glenn burst into laughter. "My sister? She'd drive an abductor to distraction with her incessant chatter. He'd be paying *me* to take her off his hands."

"But it isn't like her to leave running the shop to her assistant for more than a few hours at a time."

Glenn frowned. "True." He tapped his phone against his leg. "Don't worry. I'll track her down."

Carol returned to the kitchen, fighting a fresh knot of anxiety in her head.

An hour later, Molly slipped into the kitchen and made a show of hiding around the corner. "What do I do? He's going to recognize me."

"Who?" Carol poked her head out the door and glanced toward the café but couldn't see who Molly was talking about.

"Steve." Molly's eyes went wide. "He's here. He must've heard Angus barking when he approached the shop and detoured to the fenced yard. I spotted him when I went to warn Angus to shush." Molly anxiously eyed the hallway beyond the door. "Steve was making a huge fuss over Angus. I heard him say, 'I know you. Where's your owner?'"

"Wait here." Carol went out to the front of the bakery and approached Steve, who had just entered. "Hello. Steve, isn't it?"

He smiled in recognition. "That's right."

"Glad you could come by."

He hitched his thumb toward the yard. "I think I know that Scottie's owner." He scanned the seating area. "But I don't see her here."

"Molly? She lives upstairs." Carol could've sworn she heard Molly's groan emanate from the kitchen.

"Long blonde bangs that get into her blue eyes?" As Steve described her, a whimsical grin curved his lips. "Brilliant smile?"

Carol fought down a grin of her own. "Yes. Sounds like her."

"We met at the dog park a few days ago. She's friends with a woman I was hoping to connect with."

Carol cocked her head. Did he really not know the missing woman he'd spent the previous afternoon searching for was the same Jeanette? "Small world. By the way, I didn't get a chance to thank you yesterday for joining in the search for Jeanette."

"Jeanette," he repeated, then his complexion blanched. "Is the missing woman—Jeanette—Molly's friend?"

Carol nodded solemnly, pretty sure the horror on his ashen face couldn't be faked.

"I guess that explains why she never showed," he rasped.

"Pardon me?"

"It's nothing. I just didn't realize I kind of know the missing woman too." He turned to leave.

"Didn't you come in for something?" Carol went around the counter. "We're still pretty well stocked for a Saturday."

"Oh." Steve seemed to rally. "Yes. I'll take one of the blueberry muffins and a couple dozen shortbread cookies."

"A sweet tooth, eh?" Carol grabbed a pre-filled box of shortbread from a display stack.

His smile didn't reach his eyes. "I volunteer at a youth center and thought I'd share."

"In that case." Carol opened the box and added a few more cookies. "The extras are on the house."

"Thanks," Steve said as he handed over money.

While Carol was counting out Steve's change, Molly emerged from the kitchen with a sheepish expression.

Steve pocketed the money and hurried toward her. "I'm so sorry. I just heard about your friend, Jeanette. I joined the search for her yesterday but hadn't made the connection she was your friend." He sighed. "I must have subconsciously hoped it wouldn't be the same Jeanette. Have you heard anything more?"

Molly shook her head. "No new leads."

Carol came around the counter with the bagged muffin and box of cookies. "How did it go with your boys on the search yesterday?"

"Sorry we left so quickly." Steve pulled a face. "One of the lads tangled himself in poison oak."

"How awful," Molly said, patting Steve's arm sympathetically.

With a jingle of the bell, Fergus entered the bakery at that moment and immediately scanned the room. His gaze collided with Molly's, but the smile on his lips faded as he caught sight of her hand on Steve's arm. Fergus detoured to the counter, ordered a muffin to go from a newly arrived Bridget, then waved in their direction as he hurried out.

"I ought to go too," Steve said, taking his purchases from Carol. "See you around."

Carol chuckled after the door closed behind him. "If I didn't know better, I'd say Fergus seemed a tad jealous. Don't you think?"

Molly rolled her eyes. "*Yer heid's full o' mince*," she growled, imitating a Scottish drawl. "We're just friends."

"Me thinks the lass protests too much," Carol said airily, then returned to the kitchen.

As she began collecting ingredients for her next recipe, she considered Steve's show of surprise at learning that Jeanette from Puppy Love and the missing Jeanette were the same person. Had the reaction been genuine? Deciding to cover all bases, she texted Officer Drummond about Steve's meeting Jeanette through the website as well as his connection to Mr. Franklin's business. The policeman sent back a succinct response about checking into it.

Sometime later, Bridget popped her head into the kitchen. "It's him. He's here."

"Who's here now?" Laura asked.

"The investigator Mr. Franklin hired."

Wiping the flour from their hands, Carol and Laura hurried out to the counter with Bridget. The man was average height and average weight, wearing the same kind of chinos and casual shirt half the tourists wore. His eyes were an unexceptional matte brown, and his complexion was mildly tanned. He had no facial hair, and the locks on his head were neither too long nor too short. All to say, he looked totally ordinary, unremarkable, and unmemorable, which, Carol supposed, was exactly what a PI trying to blend into the background would want.

"Have you found Jeanette?" Carol asked.

"I see Bridget has told you who I am," the man said. "And no, my investigation is still in its early stages. Annemarie tells me you spoke with a man who corresponded with her mother. Can you tell me about him?"

Molly, who had just finished helping a customer, filled him in on what they'd learned about Steve, and the PI intermittently asked detailed questions.

But there was something about the questions that made Carol wonder what, exactly, he'd been hired to do. Was Jack Franklin afraid suspicion would increasingly shift to him and had hired a PI to make himself look like a worried husband—instead of one with something to hide?

Then again, maybe she was overreacting. She'd suspected Steve herself, after all.

"Are you questioning all the local businessmen specializing in climate control?" Carol asked. "It seems they all have ample motive to block Franklin's deal."

"That's one potential way to see it," the investigator said with a smirk, the first indication that he wasn't necessarily as bland as his appearance made him seem. "Then there are some women who, being in a vindictive state of mind, might orchestrate such a disappearance themselves."

Bridget gasped, but Carol couldn't totally fault the man for the theory. Years of meeting her pupils' parents, many of whom were divorced, had left her with no illusions about how far a spurned spouse might go. But in the Franklins' case, it'd sounded as if the separation had been Jeanette's idea. One thing was for sure—Carol was glad Annemarie wasn't here to hear what the PI had insinuated about her mother. Carol glanced toward the customers sitting at the tables on the other side of the room. Fortunately, none of them seemed to be paying any attention to the conversation.

Carol fixed an appraising eye on the PI. Maybe if he was just looking for ways to keep his client's reputation clean, he could come in handy investigating another lead. "While you're snooping around," she said, "you might want to look into Henry Roberts, the owner of The Artful Codger. He was in possession of Scout's dog tag, although he claimed he found it Tuesday, which we have no way to verify."

"Yeah," Molly chimed in. "And it seems awfully suspicious that less than half a day after Carol asked Doreen Giobsan to find out if the man owns a dog, she disappeared on an impromptu vacation. Especially when Doreen's been speculating for weeks that there's something not exactly on the up-and-up about his business."

Carol cocked her head. Why hadn't she thought to mention that when Drummond had asked if Henry had motive? She pressed her lips together. Because she hadn't put much stock in Doreen's speculation. But what if there was something to it? After Jeanette overheard Doreen complaining, she'd been quite concerned her purchase from Henry's store might've been stolen. Maybe Jeanette had decided to check it out for herself—and asked one too many questions.

"You're referring to Doreen Giobsan, the owner of Thistle and That?" the PI asked Molly.

"That's right."

His eyes narrowed. "How well did Doreen know Jeanette?"

Molly shrugged. "I have no idea."

Laura planted her hands on her hips. "You can't possibly think Doreen had anything to do with Jeanette's disappearance."

"Doreen's brother owns B&G's," the PI said. "It's one of Franklin's biggest competitors."

Laura blanched. "Doreen borrowed money from her brother to do her shop renovations—a loan she might be having difficulty paying back given her recent sales slump." Laura gave herself a shake, her expression suddenly horrified that she'd shared that information with the investigator.

"Unless she paid her dues to him another way," the PI said, his smirk now firmly fixed to his face. He tucked his notepad and pencil in his shirt pocket and mimed tipping an invisible hat. "Thank you for your help, ladies."

When the door shut behind him, Laura stomped her foot. Carol could envision steam bursting from her ears. "I can't believe I told him that about Doreen. There's no way she'd hurt Jeanette."

"I agree," Carol said.

Molly snapped her fingers. "But what if she enticed Jeanette out of town? I've got an idea where Doreen might've sent her."

"Where?" Laura and Carol asked.

"That retreat center Doreen went to last fall and couldn't stop raving about," Molly answered, growing more excited about the idea. "Paradise Sanctuary. She said it was a place to get away from life's everyday stresses and immerse oneself in prayer and quiet reflection. Remember?"

"I remember," Bridget said. "No electronics were allowed on the grounds. I wouldn't survive a day."

"And that means she wouldn't have her phone to get Annemarie's calls." Carol's hopes lifted. "I think you might be on to something. I remember Doreen mentioning the retreat while Jeanette was here, and maybe Jeanette asked her about it. We should go check it out right after closing."

Hamish, who'd taken over counter duties while the women were answering the PI's questions, crossed his arms. "Why don't you tell that PI to check it out?" he asked. "That's what he's being paid to do, isn't it?"

Carol, Laura, and Molly all stared at him as if he'd grown a third ear. "Isn't it obvious?" Laura asked. "We don't trust him."

13

The bakery had been unusually quiet since the lunch rush, probably because it was so hot and all the tourists were swarming the ice cream trucks instead. Carol glanced at her watch for the fifteenth time. *Why does time always seem to crawl when you least want it to?*

Hamish, about to head home at the end of his shift, took off the cap he'd just put on and fixed his blue eyes on Carol. "You hens get going to that retreat center you suspect Jeanette might be at. Bridget and I can mind the shop for the last hour before closing."

Carol's spirits lifted. "Are you sure?"

"Aye. You know Joyce doesn't want me underfoot while she's teaching piano lessons anyway. She'd see it as a favor if you kept me out of the house until dinnertime."

"I'll drive," Laura volunteered, clearly not willing to give Hamish time to take back his offer. She held up her phone. "I already pulled up directions."

A few minutes later, the Bakehouse Three were settled in the red Volkswagen Beetle. Carol usually enjoyed driving around with the convertible's top down, but they all agreed that the hot, humid day called for air-conditioned comfort. Apparently the ride was so comfortable that, somewhere between the stop sign at the end of the first block and the edge of town, Carol's restless night caught up to her and she dozed off. The next thing she knew, Laura was navigating onto a serene, tree-lined lane into the spacious grounds of Paradise Sanctuary. Carol sat up and stretched the kink from her neck.

Quaint cottages were scattered about the grounds, each surrounded by its own copse of trees. Gardens of every description—a water garden, a rose garden, a rock garden, an herb garden—dotted the spaces between, connected by curving pebbled pathways through swaths of lawn that were surprisingly green, considering how hot and dry the summer had been.

"This place looks so peaceful," Carol said as Laura parked outside the main central building. According to a posted sign, this housed the reception area, a gift shop, a chapel, and the refectory.

The reception area had glass walls that arched into a domed ceiling, giving it the look and feel of a solarium, minus the heat.

A cheery, young brunette behind the desk greeted them brightly. "Welcome to Paradise!" She wore a dark green polo shirt with *Paradise Sanctuary* emblazoned over her heart, likely the staff uniform.

Molly veered off toward a giant diorama of the retreat center while Carol and Laura approached the receptionist.

"Thank you, Amanda," Carol said, reading her name tag. "The place is beautiful."

"I'm glad you think so. Do you wish to book a stay with us? We're at capacity at the moment"—Amanda scanned an appointment book on the counter in front of her—"but we have a vacancy coming available next Thursday."

"Actually, we were hoping you could give us some information," Carol said. "We're looking for a woman named Jeanette Franklin, and we have reason to believe she might be here."

Amanda's demeanor cooled perceptibly. "I'm sorry. You must understand our clients' privacy is of the utmost importance. I couldn't possibly divulge such information."

"But surely you've seen on the news her fam—"

"No. Cell phones, TVs, radios, and computers are all prohibited here."

"That's the problem," Laura interjected. "If Jeanette's here, like we think, she'd have no idea how worried her family is about her welfare."

"I'm sorry." The receptionist walked around the counter and motioned them toward the exit.

Molly sauntered toward Amanda as if Laura and Carol were strangers. "Perhaps you can help me. I'm interested in staying here for a few days, but I'd like a tour before I make a reservation."

In an instant, the receptionist was all smiles once more. "Of course! I can arrange a tour immediately if now would suit."

"That's perfect," Molly agreed.

"Oh, I've always wanted to stay here," Laura piped up, her earlier testiness melting away. "Would it be all right if my friend and I tag along?"

Amanda narrowed her eyes, clearly suspicious of Laura's motives. But after a moment, her smile brightened. "Yes of course." She pressed a buzzer and a bubbly blonde appeared. She looked to be about Bridget's age and wore a green polo shirt that matched Amanda's.

"These ladies would like a tour of the grounds," Amanda announced loudly enough for them all to hear, then leaned close to the newcomer's ear and added something more softly.

Carol suspected she was being warned they were after information about a guest.

The blonde offered them a warm smile. "Good afternoon, ladies. I'm Polly and I'll be your tour guide. We'll start with the refectory, where we provide our guests with three delicious and nutritious meals a day." She motioned toward a hall at the rear of the lobby. "If you'll follow me this way."

As the trio fell into step behind their tour guide, Carol whispered to Laura and Molly, "We need to keep our eyes open for Jeanette and be careful how we ask questions. We don't want Polly to cut our tour short."

"What time is supper served?" Laura asked their tour guide, no doubt thinking that visiting the refectory during mealtime would be the surest way to spot Jeanette.

"Six o'clock." Polly pointed out the salad bar and drink station as they passed through. "But we always have healthy snacks available." At the side of the building, near the main entrance to the refectory, she indicated a table laden with a selection of fruit, nuts, and granola bars.

Unfortunately, it was hours before dinner. Aside from an elderly couple enjoying a cup of tea, the area was devoid of guests.

Polly led them through the chapel next, and Molly's phone chose that moment to beep an alarm. "I'll have to insist you turn off your phones while you're here," Polly scolded mildly. "Electronics are strictly prohibited on the grounds, as they would disturb the guests' solitude."

"Sorry, it's my monthly alarm to remind me to give Angus his heartworm pill." Molly scrambled to silence her phone before it went off again.

Laura and Carol muted their phones as well, though Carol noticed that they didn't have service anyway.

As Polly led them outside, Carol braced herself for the assault of heat and humidity, but somehow, the heat wave the entire Upper Peninsula had been enduring for the past few days didn't seem as intense in Paradise.

"All the trees have been strategically planted to offer an ample selection of shady spots for quiet contemplation and reflection," Polly explained as she led them past a beautiful water feature.

A soft breeze rustled through the trees. Carol inhaled, savoring the lovely scent of roses and freesia. Despite not being far from a main road, traffic noise was surprisingly muted. Instead, the relaxing sound of birds tweeting and water babbling filled the air. It was incredibly peaceful.

Carol spotted several guests enjoying various shady spots about the grounds—one reading, one painting, one snoozing, another writing in a journal. Jeanette wasn't among them. Thinking of Scout, who they'd already determined wasn't being boarded locally, Carol asked, "Do you allow guests to bring pets?"

"Sorry, no," Polly answered tightly, as though it should be obvious that dogs would interrupt the serenity.

"Oh, Angus wouldn't be happy about that," Molly said.

"I understand," Polly said. "And we recognize that being separated from one's pet is difficult for some people, but animals are too unpredictable and potentially disruptive to the solitude of other guests. Certified therapy animals, of course, are exempt from this restriction."

"Of course," Carol murmured, but since Scout didn't qualify for such an exemption, it was becoming increasingly doubtful Jeanette was here.

"For example," Polly went on, "just the other day, a bedraggled little dog darted in front of one of our housekeepers' cars. Assuming it was lost, she tried to coax it into her car to take to a shelter, but the silly thing refused her compassion and dashed off toward the woods, only to run out at her car all over again when she climbed back in."

"It sounds as if the dog wanted her to follow him." Carol's breath caught. "What kind of dog was it?"

Polly shrugged. "She didn't say."

Laura, Carol, and Molly exchanged stunned glances. Carol understood that electronics were forbidden on the premises, but surely employees watched the news or read the paper—wouldn't the woman have recognized Scout?

"Where's this housekeeper now?" Molly asked.

Polly frowned, confusion mingling with suspicion on her face.

"We need to talk to her," Carol explained. "You must've seen on the news that the police are looking for a missing local woman and her dog—a springer spaniel. Your housekeeper might have seen that dog. She could have vital information that could help the police find them."

Polly's eyes widened. "Yes, I did hear about it, but it never occurred . . ." Her gaze darted to the main building. "Follow me. If we hurry, we should be able to catch Lisa in the laundry room before she leaves for the day."

As they neared the main building, a handful of women exited and headed for the parking lot. "Lisa, wait up," Polly called, and a brunette stopped and glanced over her shoulder at them.

"These women have a couple of questions about the dog that ran at your car," Polly said as she and the Bakehouse Three reached the housekeeper.

Lisa's eyes filled with sympathy. "Did your dog run away?"

"Not our dog," Laura said. "A friend's. Do you know what kind of dog you saw?"

"It wasn't too big. Brown and white with floppy ears."

"That could be a spaniel," Polly said.

Carol pulled up the photo of Jeanette and Scout that she had saved on her phone. "Was it this dog?"

Lisa peered at the screen but shrugged. "Maybe, but I don't really know. His coat was matted with burrs, and it looked like he needed a good meal. I figured he had been lost for a while. He was friendly enough, but when I tried to urge him into my car, he got really skittish and dashed back toward the woods."

"Where was this?" Carol asked.

Lisa shifted her stance, orienting herself to the parking lot exit. "You take a left out of the lot and turn left at the second stop sign. It was about a mile down that road. There's not much out that way but vegetation."

The women thanked Polly and Lisa for their help, then immediately drove to the area Lisa had seen the dog. Laura parked about a mile down the old country road.

Carol squinted at the woods on either side of the road. "Did Lisa say which side of the road the dog had come from?"

"I don't think so," Molly said.

"We'll have to scout both sides then. I'll head south. You two can walk north." Carol cupped her hands around her mouth. "Scout! Here, boy!"

Molly and Laura did the same, headed in the other direction.

When they met back at the car an hour later, Carol asked, "Did you see paw prints anywhere?"

Both Molly and Laura shook their heads. "I'm afraid if it was Scout, he's long gone now," Laura said.

"Someone else might've managed to coax him into their car," Molly said. "We're far enough out of Loch Mallaig here that he might've been taken to a shelter further afield."

Carol heaved a sigh. "I'm pretty sure Bridget and Annemarie connected with every shelter they could find a number for in the Upper Peninsula."

"Sure, but now we know Scout wasn't wearing a dog tag. That could have caused problems," Laura said.

"Or maybe someone decided to keep him since he didn't have a tag," Molly theorized. "Although you'd think they'd come forward if they saw his picture on TV."

"Not necessarily," Laura countered. "One thing we haven't really considered is that lots of people these days don't watch the local networks, just their favorite shows on streaming services."

"Ugh," Molly said. "I hadn't really thought of that."

"So." Carol stared across the road at the thick stretch of brush. "What do we do now?"

14

After a few moments of contemplation, Carol pulled out her smartphone. "We should look up the vets in this area. If Scout's rescuer opted to keep him, hopefully he or she would have had him checked out. It sounds like he was in rough shape when Lisa saw him."

They all climbed back into Laura's Beetle and searched the Internet on their phones for addresses of local vets.

"There are more than half a dozen in the area," Molly said.

"Let's start with the ones closest to here," Carol said. She called the two nearest vet clinics, but nobody answered the phone at either one. They decided to stop by instead. Laura punched the address of the closest one into her GPS, and less than ten minutes later they pulled into the vet's parking lot.

Dogs in outdoor kennels barked excitedly as the women stepped out of the car. Molly and Laura headed for the main door, but Carol took a detour toward the kennels. Unfortunately, there was no sign of any spaniels among the animated canines, so she rejoined the other women.

Once inside, Molly asked the matronly receptionist if anyone had recently brought in a spaniel.

The receptionist paused as if searching her memory. "No, I can't remember the last time we saw a spaniel in here."

The scene repeated itself at the next vet's office.

"Let's check out the veterinary clinic northwest of town," Laura said as she input the address to the GPS, her voice more optimistic than Carol felt.

The GPS had them weaving from one unfamiliar rural back road to another.

"Hey." Molly pointed to a vehicle pulling out onto the road ahead of them. "Isn't that Henry Roberts's delivery truck?"

Laura slowed her car as they approached the rutted lane the man had just exited. "Maybe Doreen was right about him buying hot merchandise. This remote place would be perfect for conducting a transaction undetected."

"Or he made a wrong turn," Carol said.

"Onto that road?" Molly scoffed. "I doubt he could wind up all the way out here by accident. Let's check it out."

Laura turned down the road, which wasn't quite as bad as it had appeared at the intersection. At least not until they reached an overgrown field. Laura stopped the car and shifted into park. "Dead end."

"I think that's an old logging road." Molly pointed. "It looks like a car has been down it recently."

"A truck maybe," Laura said. "I'm not risking it. My car is too low to clear the weeds."

But Henry's truck could've cleared them. Carol squinted in the direction of the disappearing tracks. Suddenly Laura's joke about him dealing in stolen goods didn't seem so amusing. Carol jumped out of the car and scanned the ground. There were no signs of paw prints or shoe prints, and Jeanette couldn't have tracked Henry up the farmer's lane in her Saab any better than Laura could have in the Beetle.

Returning to the car, Carol dug in her purse for a map from the search party, which pinpointed trailheads in the area. None were anywhere near where she estimated this unmarked road to be. Still . . .

Carol went back toward the tracks. "Scout," she called loudly. "You here, boy? Come, Scout!"

The woods stood silent. Not so much as a rustle disturbed the quiet.

Molly climbed out of the car. "I think you were right about Henry just making a wrong turn. From the way the ground is chewed up, it looks as if he turned his truck around here." She pointed to the grooves in the dirt. "And besides our tracks, there only seems to be one other set. Wider ones, like Henry's truck."

Laura stuck her head partway out her window. "If we don't get a move on, we might not reach the next vet office before it closes for the day."

It was a good thing they hurried. At the vet, located five miles outside of Loch Mallaig, they hit pay dirt.

"Somebody brought in an injured spaniel he found this morning," the tech manning the desk told them. His name tag identified him as Nick. "The dog is currently sedated, but you're welcome to take a look at him to see if he belongs to your friend."

The trio followed the friendly young man down a long hallway to a sterile-feeling room full of empty cages, save one. In it was a sleeping spaniel who resembled Scout. But instead of the shiny coat they were used to seeing, his fur was dirty and matted.

"Is he your friend's?" Nick asked.

Carol held up the picture of Scout and glanced from it to the dog in the cage. The injured dog had three white legs and one brown, like Scout. The coloring on its muzzle appeared the same too. But with this dog's fur as badly matted as it was, it was difficult to tell if the rest of his markings were identical. Molly, Laura, and even the vet tech compared the picture to the sedated dog, but they all reached the same nonconclusion.

"Maybe we should ask Annemarie to come down and see for herself," Laura suggested. "Or are you closing now?"

"We are," Nick said. "But go ahead and call her. I have at least half an hour's worth of work to finish before I leave."

"They should be able to get here by then," Carol said as she dialed Annemarie.

She and Bridget wasted no time getting to the clinic. Nick ushered them all back into the recovery room, where he opened the cage so Annemarie could get closer to the dog.

Annemarie lifted his front paw and dipped her head to peer closer. She burst into tears. "It's him. It's Scout. He has these freckles on the back of his leg."

Nick stooped down and examined the dog's paw. "That is unique. Well, I'm glad we know who this fella belongs to now."

Carol swallowed hard and exchanged wary glances with Molly and Laura. Identifying Scout was good news in one way, but Carol feared it meant something horrible had happened to Jeanette while she was out with her dog. And since Scout was sedated, he couldn't exactly lead them to her.

"Did the person who brought Scout in say where he found him?" Carol asked Nick.

"I don't know," he replied. "Why?"

Annemarie backed away from Scout and swiped her eyes with her sleeve. "My mom was walking with him and she's still missing."

Nick cringed. "I'm so sorry. I didn't realize. Our receptionist has gone home for the day, but if you don't mind waiting a moment, I can call her to see if she knows. She was the one who spoke with the guy who brought your dog in."

Molly gave Annemarie a warm hug as they waited for the vet tech's answer. "This is a good sign. Keep your hopes up. We're getting closer to finding your mom. You'll see."

Nick returned, a smile on his face. "Apparently our good Samaritan found your little fellow wandering just up the road. That's why he brought him to us."

Frustration churned inside Carol. The vet's office was located in a small village of sorts, not particularly near any trailheads and far from where Lisa had spotted him, if indeed, the dog she'd seen had been Scout.

"How far could a dog like Scout walk since Wednesday?" Bridget asked Nick.

The distance he cited was daunting. Add to it the number of different directions Scout could have come from, and they were no closer to narrowing their search zone, except perhaps to restrict it to areas west of Loch Mallaig.

"Scout should be able to go home tomorrow," Nick said. "His back leg is injured, but our vet is out on an emergency call and won't be able to check on the leg again until this evening. I'll also ensure we wash and brush him before he goes home."

Annemarie appeared as if she might burst into tears again at the idea of leaving Scout behind.

"We'll take good care of him," Nick reassured her.

Annemarie sniffed, but nodded.

As they all walked out of the building, Bridget said, "We should go up the road to where Nick said the guy found Scout and see if we can pick up his trail."

Laura smiled encouragingly. "We spoke to another person earlier who'd also tried to rescue Scout, but he wouldn't go with her. It sounded to me as if he was trying to lead her into the woods, which makes me think he could lead us to Jeanette."

A teenage boy emerged from behind the veterinary building, walking four dogs and struggling to keep their leads from tangling.

"Except the road where Lisa saw Scout—if it was Scout—was miles from here," Molly pointed out. "And we have no idea if this is closer to where Jeanette is, or if where Scout was spotted two days ago is. And he's in no condition to lead us."

"I'll call Officer Drummond and let him know we found Scout," Carol said. "Maybe he's had more tips from people who saw Jeanette's Saab that can help us narrow in on where to search."

The teen who was passing by with the dogs came to a halt. "Are you talking about the missing woman whose car was stolen by Cedric Button?"

The dead car thief? Carol swallowed her surprise. "Did you see the car?"

"No, I saw the news report," he answered as he tried to keep a large German shepherd from jumping on Bridget. "But I know Cedric. He used to hang out with my oldest brother and a guy named Jimmy Walker."

"Do you think your brother might know where Cedric was Wednesday night?" Carol asked.

"No, sorry. He joined the army and shipped out last month. But Jimmy might."

"Do you know where we can find him?" Laura asked.

The boy shrugged and pointed up the road. "His folks live in the house with the purple door on Fennel Street. I don't know if Jimmy still lives there."

Carol reached out and shook the boy's hand. "Thank you for your help."

His face reddened, and he slanted a shy look in Annemarie's and Bridget's directions. Then he gathered up the dog's leads and resumed his walk.

"Bridget," Molly said, "why don't you and Annemarie search for signs of Scout's tracks up the road, like you'd suggested, while we see if we can find this Jimmy Walker?"

The girls appeared ready to protest.

"We'll call you the second we learn anything," Carol promised.

"We don't want to scare him off by too many of us showing up on his doorstep."

The pair begrudgingly agreed, so Carol, Molly, and Laura piled back in the Beetle and drove in the direction the dog walker had indicated. Fennel Street ended at the main road they were on, so there was only one way to turn, and they soon found the house with the purple door. But a weathered *Sold* sign standing crookedly at the corner of the property indicated that the Walkers no longer lived there.

Laura stopped in front of the driveway. "The mailbox says Moore. What do you want to do?"

"I'll ask the new owners if they know where the Walkers moved to," Carol offered. She trudged up the front steps and knocked on the door repeatedly, but no one answered. Returning to the car, she pulled out her phone. "No one's home, but I have another idea. I know someone from graduate school who teaches in this school district. It's a long shot, but if she had Jimmy or any of his siblings in her class, she might know where the Walkers live now."

Carol's friend Susie answered on the third ring. "Carol? What a surprise! How are you enjoying your retirement?"

"Loving it," Carol replied. "I've actually opened a bakehouse in Loch Mallaig with a couple of friends from college."

"Loch Mallaig? Why, we're practically neighbors. I'll have to come by and check it out."

"I'd love that," Carol said honestly. "But right now, I'm hoping you can help us locate a young man who might've been a student of yours. Jimmy Walker?"

"Oh, I remember Jimmy," Susie said. "What did he do now? He didn't rob your shop, did he?"

"Nothing like that." Carol explained how they were looking for Jeanette, and about Jimmy's connection to the young man who stole her car.

"Ah," Susie said, her voice heavy. "Those two were thick as thieves—if you'll pardon the pun. Always in trouble. I'd never wish an end like that on either of them though. Poor Cedric."

"We're outside Jimmy's former house on Fennel, but it looks like it was sold recently."

"Jimmy's mom died in the spring. His dad has been out of the picture for years. If I had to guess, he and his brother probably moved in with their grandfather." Susie described the general vicinity of the man's rundown shack, which was within a mile of their current location. "You can't miss it. Be careful, though," she warned. "Jimmy had a few run-ins with the law as a juvenile, mostly minor stuff. But there was an assault too."

"Thanks for the heads-up. I'll be in touch soon." Carol relayed the directions Susie had given to the grandfather's home, and Laura started down Fennel Street.

"I called Officer Drummond to update him on finding Scout and the tip about Jimmy Walker," Molly said as they drove.

"What did he say?"

"He said he'd let Sheriff Bugle know."

Carol raised an eyebrow. "You didn't tell him we were looking Jimmy up?"

Molly laughed. "And risk him telling us to stand down?"

Laura stopped the car. "You might want to rethink leaving the questioning to the cops." She jutted her chin toward a dilapidated house on a patch of weedy dirt. "That's the grandfather's place."

The roof over the front porch appeared ready to cave in on the dirt-smeared boy sitting on the step whittling a stick.

"Park here," Carol said. "I'll walk across the yard."

The house was the only one within sight on the rural road. Spindly dead trees surrounded the place, making it seem like something out of an apocalypse movie.

"Hello," Carol called to the boy. "Is this the Walker place?"

The boy closed his jackknife and stuffed it in his pocket. "Who wants to know?"

Carol introduced herself. "I'm looking for Jimmy Walker. I'm hoping he can help me locate a friend. Is he your brother?"

"Yeah. But he ain't home yet."

Carol chose her next question carefully, hoping to avoid causing the boy to clam up. "Is he still at work?"

The boy shrugged.

"If you tell me where he works, I could try there."

"Steve's. He delivers stuff for him."

Carol's heart missed a beat. "Steve's? As in Gambel's Heating and Air?"

"Yeah."

It couldn't be a coincidence. Carol glanced at the home's grimy windows and broken blinds beyond. Then again, Jimmy was probably exactly the kind of young man Steve would take under his wing.

"That's great," she managed. "I'll try him there." She started toward the car but stopped, deciding to try one last question. "Do you happen to know if Jimmy went out with Cedric Button Wednesday night?"

The boy sprang to his feet and nervously backed toward the house's front door. "I ain't supposed to say."

"I know they were good friends," Carol said sympathetically, hoping to reassure him she wasn't looking to get anyone in trouble. "Jimmy must be upset over losing him."

The boy nodded.

Carol waited, sensing he was itching to say more.

An old man tromped around the side of the house, a distinctively sour smell clinging to his grimy clothes. "A pretty lady pays a visit and you don't offer her a drink?" he growled. "Where are your manners, boy?"

"She was asking about Jimmy, Grandpa."

The old man peered at Carol through rheumy eyes. "It's about time that lad found himself a girl." He had clearly mistaken her for Jimmy's sweetheart. Apparently his vision was too poor to see she was more than twice Jimmy's age. "Fetch her a lemonade," he said to the boy, then lowered himself into a creaky rocking chair.

Carol was about to object, then decided she might glean more information from the grandfather if the boy wasn't around to shush him. "Thank you. A glass of lemonade sounds nice." After the boy disappeared inside, she turned back to his grandfather. "You wouldn't happen to know where Jimmy and his friend Cedric went Wednesday night, would you?"

He shook his head. "The boy is too old to answer to me about where he goes at night. But I wager he won't be doing it again soon."

"Why's that?" Carol asked.

He raised a scraggly, gray eyebrow. "Didn't Jimmy show you his gunshot wound?"

15

Carol gaped at Jimmy Walker's grandfather. "Jimmy was shot?"

"Yup." Jimmy's grandfather leaned back in his rickety chair with a prolonged creak. "Only grazed the shoulder, mind you. Patched it up himself," he added, almost sounding proud. "I wouldn't have known nothing about it, except I don't sleep more than a few winks a night."

"Did he say who shot him?"

"Nope. Didn't want to get a friend in trouble, I expect. I remember playing with air rifles myself as a boy. But this'll teach him to respect the gun's power."

"Did Jimmy mention being in a car accident Wednesday night?"

Jimmy's younger brother emerged from the house and, given his tight-fisted grip on the lemonade glass he held, Carol suspected he knew something about the crash.

"Car accident?" The old man's brow furrowed. "No."

Jimmy thrust the lemonade into Carol's hand. "I'm going to play at Andy's," he blurted to his grandpa, then dashed toward the road.

For the first time, Carol noticed a young man perched on a bicycle several car lengths behind Laura's Beetle.

The younger boy spoke to him, and an instant later, the rider turned his bike around and took off.

"Does Jimmy ride a bike to work?" Carol asked the old man.

"A bike? Yeah, sometimes. If his friend can't give him a lift."

Carol set down her glass of lemonade. "Thank you for your time, Mr. Walker. I need to go now."

The elderly man pushed to his feet. "Don't you want to wait for Jimmy? He shouldn't be much longer."

"No thanks. I really need to go." Carol dashed to the car. Laura had it started before Carol slid into the passenger seat. "Follow that cyclist. I think it was Jimmy."

"You got it." Laura pulled a smooth U-turn, then surged forward.

"This case is getting more convoluted by the minute," Carol said. "Someone shot Jimmy Wednesday night. If he was with Cedric, then maybe their car accident was no accident. And his little brother knows more than he's saying too. I'm sure of it."

"Someone shot at them?" Molly repeated from the back seat. "So you think they saw something someone didn't want them talking about?"

"Maybe." Carol pointed to the bend in the road ahead. "There he is. Slow down. Don't spook him." Carol whirred open her window as they reached him. "Jimmy, we need to talk to you." She was so close to him that she could've reached out the window and grabbed his handlebars.

Jimmy glanced at her, then veered off the road through the trees.

"Stop!" Carol cried, as much to Jimmy as Laura. Carol jumped out of the car and chased after him. But on the bike, he soon tripled and quadrupled the distance between them.

The sound of a boat engine roaring to life spurred Carol on, but by the time she burst through the trees into a clearing at the edge of Loch Mallaig, Jimmy was in a boat yards from shore, his bike unceremoniously dumped at the water's edge.

Carol clenched her fists. The kid had to know he couldn't hide forever. Meanwhile, time could be running out for Jeanette. Her heart squeezed. *If it's not already too late.*

Molly and Laura appeared at Carol's side, and Carol pointed toward the water. "He's out there."

Molly had her cell phone pressed to her ear. "He's out on the lake in a motorboat," she said into the phone. "He's got to know something. Why else would he run?" She ended her call. "Officer Drummond is sending a police boat to collect Jimmy and someone to talk to the little brother. He's already called Sheriff Bugle and asked him to compare Jimmy's prints with others found in the car."

"Good," Laura said. "If they find his prints, the police will have more leverage to convince Jimmy to talk."

As the trio trudged out of the bush back to their car, Carol's phone beeped a text message notification. She glanced at the phone's screen. "It's Bridget. She says they had no luck finding a trail and she wants to know if Jimmy told us anything."

Not yet. Carol responded.

The phone beeped again. "The girls are back at the vet's," Carol reported. "The doctor is examining Scout now."

"Tell her we'll meet them there," Laura said, starting the car.

During the drive to the vet, Carol pried off the burrs clinging to her pants. Scrutinizing one of the burrs, an idea popped into her mind. "Remember that naturalist that Hamish was chatting with at the bakehouse last week?" An avid bird-watcher, Hamish knew many other nature lovers in the area.

"Yes!" Molly leaned forward eagerly. "I think her name was Linaya. When he introduced her, he mentioned she can examine burrs and seeds found on your clothes and pretty accurately pinpoint where you've been. She's even done it to help the police solve crimes."

"Scout's fur was matted with burrs," Laura said. "Do you think Linaya could tell where he was by looking at them?"

"I think she might. It's worth a shot." Carol called Hamish to get the woman's contact information, then dialed the number, but it went to voice mail. Carol explained the situation, reiterated the urgency, then disconnected just as Laura pulled the car into the vet's parking lot.

"Isn't that Annemarie's father?" Laura gestured toward a man entering the clinic's front door.

"Annemarie must've called him about Scout," Molly said.

"It could be interesting to see how Scout reacts to him," Carol mused.

"Is he still a suspect?" Laura asked as she parked. "I can't keep up."

Carol shrugged. "Everyone is still a suspect. Since he needs Jeanette to sign the papers for the sale of his company to proceed, it doesn't make sense that he had something to do with all this. But I'm still not sure we can trust him."

"I wonder if his wife's shares revert to him if her body turns up," Molly said, unbuckling her seat belt.

Carol shivered. "Could be. It would alleviate the need for her signature."

They hurried inside, but found the waiting room and receptionist desk empty.

Molly poked her head down the hallway. "Hello?"

Bridget stepped out of a room at the end of the hall and motioned for them to follow.

When the women reached the door of the room, they heard a male voice saying, "He should be able to put weight on the leg within twenty-four to thirty-six hours. But it'll likely be a week or two before he's back to his normal self."

"Can I take him home now?" Annemarie asked.

"Of course," the vet said. "He'll be a little sluggish for a few more hours due to the sedation. Give him only a small meal tonight and another in the morning."

Annemarie's father gently scooped Scout into his arms and the dog licked the man's hand.

Not the response a dog would have to his mistress's attacker.

"Do you want to sit in the back with him?" Mr. Franklin asked Annemarie.

"I have my car here," she said. "You can put him in my back seat and Bridget can drive."

The man frowned, but didn't protest before carrying Scout out of the room.

"Scout doesn't seem to think he's a bad guy," Molly whispered to Carol and Molly as they watched the procession head out the door.

"Or he's still too sedated to recognize him," Laura said.

Carol tugged aside Nick, the vet tech they'd spoken with earlier. "Do you still have the burrs you combed from the dog's fur?"

He gave Carol a peculiar look. "They're in the garbage pail in the examination room. Why?"

"I'd like to take them. We know someone who might be able to figure out where he's been by"—Carol clammed up as Mr. Franklin returned, his credit card in hand.

"I thought I'd settle the bill before we go," he told Nick.

"Of course." Nick rounded the desk and tapped a few computer keys. He glanced at Carol. "Exam room four. You can take the whole bag. There's nothing else in it."

Carol nodded her thanks and hurried down the hall. Finding the right room, she let herself in. Sure enough, the white plastic bag lining the small stainless steel bucket had a ball of burrs and dog fur in the bottom. Carol bent down and tied the bag.

"May I help you?"

Carol jumped at the veterinarian's voice, but recovered quickly and explained why she wanted the bag.

"Interesting," Dr. Vail said. "I don't know if it would help your naturalist friend's findings, but I also found a large splinter in the dog's paw pad. It wasn't from living wood though. It appeared more like an old barn board or fallen fence board."

"Thank you." Carol nodded. "That could prove very helpful." *At least I hope it will.* If it didn't, Carol knew, Jeanette's time could run out . . . if it hadn't already.

Weary and hungry after the eventful afternoon, Carol arrived home ready for dinner and an early night. But two other cars besides Harvey's lined the driveway. Recognizing one as Jenny's minivan, she groaned and hurried out of the car.

"I'm so sorry," Carol said as Jenny rounded the corner of the house, her long dark hair bobbing in a ponytail. "I got caught up with helping Bridget's friend find her mother and totally forgot our dinner plans."

Amusement twinkled in Jenny's brown eyes. "Dad told us all about it. And don't worry, he's grilling the fish he caught along with potatoes and vegetables for supper."

Carol hugged her daughter. "What would I do without your father?"

Maisie and Gavin raced across the yard and caught Carol in a three-way bear hug.

"We found eggs!" Maisie announced, her hazel eyes beaming with pride.

"Can we make cookies with them?" Gavin asked.

Carol took their hands in hers and headed toward the house. "I would love to do that."

Jenny pointed to the trash bag propped on Carol's front seat. "Is that what your friend is waiting to look at?"

"What friend?"

"Your friend Linaya. She showed up a few minutes ago."

"She's here?" Carol yelped, then collected both the bag of burrs and her wits. She returned to the kids and crouched down so her eyes were at their level. "I'm afraid our baking lesson is going to have to wait, but you might find it interesting to see what Mr. Bruce's friend can deduce about a little dog's travels by looking at the burrs brushed from his coat. Would you like to see?"

Maisie scrunched her nose, clearly not excited about the change in plans, but Gavin's eyes widened as he scoped out the contents of the bag. "Cool!"

"She's around back by the barbecue with Craig and Dad," Jenny said, leading the way.

Carol greeted her husband with a kiss and her son-in-law with a hug, then warmly welcomed Linaya, a short woman with spiky gray hair and a cherubic face. "Thank you for coming so quickly."

"I tried calling you back but didn't get an answer, so I asked Hamish for your address," Linaya explained. "It turns out we're neighbors. I live just down the road."

"I appreciate you stopping by," Carol said. "The situation is rather urgent."

"I'm happy to help," Linaya said graciously. "I heard about the missing woman on the radio. It's already been a couple of days, hasn't it?"

"Three and a half." Carol shivered involuntarily despite the evening heat.

"Oh dear. We'd better get right to it then." Linaya reached for the bag Carol held. "Is that what you have for me to examine?"

"Yes." Carol motioned toward the patio door. "Perhaps we should take it inside so we can lay it all out on a table."

Linaya nodded. "Excellent idea."

Except for the men who were monitoring the grill, they all paraded inside. Carol cleared the table and spread out a vinyl tablecloth she kept on hand for the kids' craft projects. To get a better view, the children each kneeled on chairs at the table, then leaned forward with their chins propped up on their hands.

Linaya spread the contents of the bag over the table. One by one, she picked through burrs and seeds of various shapes and sizes and explained what plants they were from and where those plants might be found. When she reached a cluster of burrs that, to Carol, looked like all the others, Linaya grinned. "These aren't as prolific in the Upper Peninsula."

She identified them by a Latin name that had Carol's mind twisting along with her grandchildren's faces.

Linaya laughed. "The important thing is there are only two areas in the Upper Peninsula where the plants grow."

"That's great news," Carol said, excitement surging. "Where?"

"The McFarlane Conservation Area is the closest to here," Linaya answered.

"Close is relative," Jenny said. "It's over 10,000 acres, mostly wild."

Carol's pulse quickened. Yes, it was a big area used by horse riders, cyclists, and hikers. But it was also close to Beamsville, and it was the zone that Henry Roberts had convinced them not to search since he claimed he'd been to the trailhead Wednesday morning and not seen any cars. More interesting was the fact that the dead-end road they'd seen his truck pull out of earlier today was within the conservation area.

"Are there old fences in the area?" Carol asked Linaya. "Because the vet also said he pulled a large sliver from the dog's paw that looked as if it came from an old fence board."

Linaya thought for a moment. "That sounds more like the second area I was thinking of."

Carol spread an Upper Peninsula map on the table and Linaya pointed to an area southwest of town. "That's closer to where Scout was found."

"Then that's where I'd concentrate the search," Linaya said.

"What did you lose?" Maisie asked, turning wide, innocent eyes on Carol.

Jenny hugged her daughter. "A woman got lost while walking her dog in the woods. That's why Daddy and I always tell you and Gavin to stay close to us."

Maisie dug her teeth into her trembling bottom lip. "It'd be so scary to be lost in the woods."

"If that ever happens to you," Linaya said, "the most important thing you should do is stop where you are and stay calm. You shouldn't walk farther because it will take your parents all that much longer to find you."

Maisie nodded vigorously. "I will. I promise."

"And when you're older," Carol added, "If you go hiking or cycling on your own or with friends rather than Mom and Dad, be sure to let them know where you plan to go and when you expect to be back. That way if you don't return, they'll know to start looking for you."

"That's why you should get us cell phones," Gavin told his mother matter-of-factly.

Jenny scowled. "You're too young for a phone. Besides, half the time they don't work in the woods."

"It's true," Carol said. "The woman we're looking for had a phone with her, but we haven't been able to reach her on it."

The patio door opened, and Harvey and Craig came inside carrying platters of food. "Supper's ready," Harvey announced.

"Would you like to stay for dinner?" Carol asked Linaya. "We have plenty."

"That's so kind of you, but I've got plans," the naturalist responded. She placed a hand on Carol's forearm. "Please let me know if you find the woman you're looking for."

"Of course. Thank you so much for your help." Carol walked Linaya out, then returned to the kitchen and glanced at the clock. "I'm afraid I'm going to need to eat and run. There's not much time left before nightfall to search for Jeanette." She showed Harvey and Craig on the map where Linaya had recommended they concentrate their efforts.

"Harvey and I can help," Craig said, then looked to his wife. "Do you mind?"

"No, of course not." Jenny cleared the map from the table and began setting out plates and cutlery. "You should go."

"I have a friend with a four-wheeler," Craig said. "I'm sure he'd be happy to meet us there so we could cover more ground."

"That's a terrific idea," Harvey said.

Carol pulled out her phone. "I'll call Officer Drummond, Molly, and Laura, and ask them to meet us at the trailhead with whoever else they can round up."

Officer Drummond didn't pick up. Carol left a message, her heart pounding by the time she disconnected. Hopefully he was busy interrogating Jimmy and learning even more precise details of Jeanette's last known location.

"No answer, huh?" Harvey asked. "Should we hold off setting out until we hear from him?"

Carol glanced out at the sun sinking much too quickly. "No. It might be too late by then."

16

As Harvey pulled off the road to park, Carol smiled at the sight of Molly, Fergus, Hamish, and Laura talking to Deputy Chief Broderick Gillespie at the trailhead. Officer Drummond must have listened to her voice mail and sent him.

Molly waved Carol, Harvey, and Craig over. "Jimmy capsized his boat and hit his head, so they're at the hospital waiting for the doctor to give Officer Drummond the okay to question him. But the deputy chief got an admission out of Jimmy's brother that Jimmy was out with Cedric Wednesday night."

"Does the boy know where they went?" Carol asked Gillespie.

"Jimmy told him they were going to a bush party," he answered. "The boy claims he doesn't know where but that they usually went to a spot on the outskirts of the McFarlane Conservation Area." He issued a disgruntled sound. "Nowhere near here, which is where your friends are saying her dog was found."

"Yes," Laura said. "But the vet tech said Scout could've wandered for miles since Wednesday."

Broderick hummed thoughtfully. Was he wondering the same as Carol—if Scout's owner was alive, how far would he have wandered from her side?

"I have a couple of officers interviewing others who, according to Jimmy's brother, might've been at the party," the deputy chief said. "But since we're here now, I'd say let's go ahead and search this area. The sun will be below the trees in no time."

"We brought lights." Fergus turned on a powerful flashlight, and Carol noticed each of the others held similar ones.

"Here's my buddy, Devin," Craig told everyone as a four-person all-terrain vehicle driven by a thirtysomething man with brown hair and an athletic build roared up.

After a brief exchange of introductions, Devin suggested they split into groups. "There are several places where the horse trails cross the hiking trails," he explained. "I can drive a different group to each point so we can cover the whole trail before nightfall."

"Good idea," the deputy chief said. "I'll start at the farthest end of the loop and follow the other side back to the start."

Craig partnered with Gillespie, and they climbed onto the ATV. Harvey and Carol paired up and offered to set out on foot from the trailhead. Molly, Fergus, and Laura offered to search another area close by while they waited for Devin to come back and drive them to a more remote spot.

From the moment Carol and Harvey stepped into the woods, it felt as if night had already fallen. Carol tugged on her sweater, thankful she'd thought to grab it. "It's been so hot the past few days," she said to her husband. "I can't believe how cool it is in here."

Harvey whacked at a mosquito on his cheek. "Yeah, between the bugs and dropping temperatures at night, your friend can't be too comfortable."

They called Jeanette's name and listened for a reply, shining their flashlights through the trees on either side of the path. In the distance, they could hear other teams also calling out her name, but the forest was silent otherwise.

By the time they all regrouped at the trailhead more than an hour later, the blackening sky had swallowed the last wisps of purple-red clouds.

"I just got word from Drummond he's interviewing Jimmy now," Deputy Chief Gillespie said. "By morning, we should have a better idea where to concentrate the search."

"I hope so." Carol hugged herself against a chill, as much from the thought of Jeanette spending another night alone in the woods as from the temperature plummeting.

"I'll meet you back here then," Devin offered, then drove off.

Everyone else trudged back to their cars feeling even more somber than they'd been when they arrived.

Harvey looked across the car seat at Carol as he turned the key in the ignition. "Do you want to go to the hospital?"

Her breath hitched.

"I know you," Harvey said. "You won't get a wink of sleep until you find out what that car thief told Drummond."

She sighed, scratching at a fresh mosquito bite on her neck. "You're right. Are you sure you don't mind?"

He reached across the seat and squeezed her hand. "Lord knows I wouldn't be able to go home if you were missing."

As Harvey drove, Carol's thoughts turned to Annemarie's father. Sure, the Bakehouse Three hadn't called him about their impromptu search . . . but why were they the ones organizing searches in the first place? If Carol were missing, Harvey would be hounding the police into action night and day and be out in the woods himself. Which begged the question: Did Jeanette's husband know she wasn't anywhere she'd be found?

"Do you think Jack Franklin knows where Jeanette is?" she asked Harvey.

It was his turn to sigh. "I don't know what to think about the man. Did he ever cough up a name for who took out his boat Wednesday morning?"

"I'm not sure, but it couldn't have been Jeanette. The harbormaster didn't see her car there that morning."

What if someone took Jeanette from the woods, leaving behind the car and dog, and then took her out in the boat? Carol thought, then immediately shook her head. That would've been too risky. Too many potential witnesses.

"We're here," Harvey announced as he entered the hospital parking lot and pulled in next to a police cruiser. "Looks like Drummond is here too."

They walked into the medical center's small but sufficient emergency care department. Carol recognized the triage receptionist as a woman from church named Marcy, who was also a regular at the bakehouse. "Hi Marcy," she said, with what she hoped was a winning smile.

"Hi Carol, Harvey," Marcy greeted brightly, then her smile turned sympathetic. "What seems to be the problem today?"

"We need to talk to Officer Drummond when he's finished interviewing Jimmy," Carol said, deciding she didn't have time to mince words.

Marcy's eyebrows lifted. Carol knew privacy laws prohibited Marcy from confirming Jimmy was a patient, let alone that he was being questioned by the police, but Carol hoped that Marcy would at least tell them if the cruiser outside didn't belong to Drummond.

Marcy dipped her head close to Carol's. "Is this about Jeanette?"

Carol's hopes rose. "Yes."

Marcy nodded. "Once he's free, I'll let him know you're waiting to see him." She pointed to the door that led to the rest of the hospital. "You can wait in the lobby."

"Thanks, Marcy," Carol said, making a mental note to give the woman a free cup of coffee on her next visit to Bread on Arrival.

Carol and Harvey sat together on a bench in the otherwise deserted lobby. It seemed like hours before Officer Drummond finally appeared. When he did, Carol leaped up and rushed over to him.

"Does Jimmy know where Jeanette is?" Carol blurted.

Drummond glanced around but seemed satisfied that no one else was present to hear what he told the MacCallans. "He claims he never saw her."

"Where did he and his friend find her car?" Carol asked.

"On Rayburn Road. Near County Road 12."

Carol opened the ever-present area map she carried in her purse. When she located the rural intersection, near the McFarlane Conservation Area, her heart thudded. "This borders the other area Hamish's friend said Scout could've picked up the unique burrs in his fur. But why would Jeanette park there? There's no trailhead."

"Jimmy claims it's where he and Cedric came racing out of the woods and found the car sitting there," Drummond said.

"Racing?" Harvey repeated. "Was someone chasing them?"

"Apparently." Drummond hesitated.

"You can't hold out on us now," Carol pressed. "We're all on the same team."

Drummond sighed. "Jimmy claims he and Cedric got turned around in the woods when they left the party, so when they heard a dog barking they figured they'd find someone's house."

"Was it Scout?" Carol couldn't control the desperate hope coloring her voice.

"They never saw the dog. They heard it yelp as if it had been kicked, and a second later they spotted a"—Drummond winced—"to use Jimmy's term, a 'nutcase walking in circles, muttering.'"

"Nutcase?" Carol exchanged a tense glance with Harvey.

Harvey folded her cold hand in his warm one. "What happened then?"

"As soon as the guy spotted Jimmy and Cedric, he yelled at them," the officer said.

"It was a man?" Carol clarified.

"Yes. Jimmy said he asked what they were doing there, and when they turned and ran rather than answer, the guy chased them."

"So he's someone in decent physical condition," Carol mused.

Drummond gave a noncommittal shrug. "Difficult to say how much their imagination was acting up in the dark. The guy never caught up to them. At least not in the woods. They eventually found their way out close to where Jeanette's old Saab was parked. Cedric hot-wired it and they drove off. But Jimmy says a truck came roaring up behind them."

"The same guy?" Carol asked.

"Jimmy couldn't say for sure, but he figures it must've been the same guy," the officer said. "They slowed down to let the truck pass, but it didn't. It rear-ended them. They sped off, and the vehicle tailgated them all the way to the next town. Seems unlikely some random guy would do that."

"Unless they cut him off when they swerved onto the road and maybe didn't realize it," Harvey suggested. "Incidents of road rage happen all the time, even in the Upper Peninsula."

"Sure," Drummond agreed. "I speculated the same thing. But Jimmy claims they'd driven a while before the guy raced up on them. In the end, it was another clip on the bumper that sent the Saab off the road in Beamsville and into the ditch."

"Could Jimmy describe the truck?" Harvey asked.

Drummond shook his head. "Wasn't even sure if it was a truck or van, just that it was a lot bigger than the Saab."

Carol frowned in thought. "If the driver was the same guy the boys stumbled upon in the woods, he's got to have a good reason to go after them. What did they see?"

"Jimmy claims they didn't see anything. But that doesn't mean the guy didn't assume they had."

Carol's mind immediately shot in several directions as she digested this new information. The only seemingly good news was that Jimmy and Cedric had been chased by a man, which meant Doreen hadn't been involved. However, thinking of Doreen led Carol to her nemesis, Henry Roberts, who had steered the search parties away from the exact area where Jeanette's car had been.

Not that he'd necessarily lied about not seeing a car parked at the trailhead—according to Jimmy, Jeanette's Saab had been parked down the road. But Carol mentally tallied Henry's search advice, plus the dog tag he'd had in his pocket, plus his presence earlier that day on a logging road near Rayburn Road—not to mention Doreen's speculation that he was involved in something illegal—and all kinds of red flags sprang up in her mind.

But the man had to be almost seventy. Could he really have chased a couple of teen boys through the bush?

That left Jeanette's husband or her would-be date, Steve, who both had more obvious motives related to their HVAC businesses. Except, Carol reminded herself, for the fact that Mr. Franklin would presumably need to produce a dead body to finalize the sale of his company without her signature.

Or maybe Jeanette's disappearance had nothing to do with the sale. Maybe Jack Franklin had caught wind of his wife fraternizing with his competition and went nuts.

"Did you hear me?" Officer Drummond asked, his tone indicating Carol had missed something important.

Carol shook her thoughts from her head. "Sorry, no. What did you say?"

"Jimmy claims the guy who ran them off the road continued to chase them on foot after they climbed out of the car," the policeman said. "He claims the blow that killed Cedric wasn't from the car wreck, but from a rifle butt."

"What?" Carol sank onto the nearest bench and gaped at Drummond, her heart pounding.

"Jimmy says Cedric stumbled and went down. Before he could get up again, the guy clobbered him."

"Was Jimmy shot?" Carol asked. "His grandfather said he was shot by an air rifle."

Drummond nodded. "He was shot, but the doctor couldn't tell by what based on the graze it left on his shoulder."

Carol suddenly felt numb and very cold. Harvey sat next to her and wrapped his arm around her. Drummond didn't have to spell it out for them to know how bad this sounded for Jeanette. If the guy at the root of her disappearance was desperate enough to shoot at young men like Jimmy and Cedric, it sure wasn't likely Jeanette was alive.

Loud voices erupted from the direction of the triage area. An instant later, Marcy plowed through the door and scanned the lobby. When her gaze locked on to Officer Drummond, she waved frantically. "That kid you were talking to just got stabbed!"

17

Carol and Harvey trailed Officer Drummond into the emergency department and practically ran into Bridget and Annemarie. "What are you doing here?" Carol asked.

"Molly called and told us the police had Jimmy in custody here at the hospital," Bridget said. "As soon as her dad heard, he hightailed it over here."

Carol glanced around. "Where is he?"

Before Bridget could answer, the ambulance bay doors slid open and a flurry of medical personnel pushed a gurney through the door. On it, Jimmy lay squirming in pain, blood seeping through the gauze a nurse was holding against his abdomen. Carol nearly did a double take. Jimmy was a patient at the hospital, so why was he coming from outside?

Annemarie's father followed the gurney in. "I know you saw my wife. Where is she? What did you do to her?" He tried to keep up with the group, but Drummond intercepted him before he could get through the security doors.

"Did you talk to him?" Mr. Franklin demanded, rounding on Drummond. "Where's my wife?"

Annemarie dashed to her father's side. "Daddy, give him a chance to tell us."

Carol turned to Bridget. "What was Jimmy doing outside?"

Bridget shrugged. "We were about to ask the receptionist where we could find Officer Drummond when a nurse dashed up and asked for him too. She said his suspect snuck out. Annemarie's father figured the nurse was talking about Jimmy and ran outside to catch him."

"Was he carrying a knife?"

"Mr. Franklin? No!" Bridget chewed on her bottom lip. "Not that I saw at least. Maybe Jimmy stole a scalpel or something before he snuck out and ended up getting it turned on himself."

While Carol surveyed the intense exchange between Drummond and Mr. Franklin, Harvey stepped over and whispered close to her ear, "I overheard Jack swear Jimmy was already bleeding when he found him doubled over outside."

At that moment, a familiar face walked through the security doors, escorting a teenage boy with his arm in a sling.

"That's Steve—the guy Jeanette was talking to online," Carol hissed to Harvey and Bridget.

"You think Jimmy saw him and that's why he bolted?" Harvey speculated.

Carol shook her head. "Steve's his boss, so unless he was afraid of him for another reason—like he was the guy in the field—seeing him here shouldn't have made him run."

"But then who stabbed Jimmy?" Bridget asked.

Carol squinted at Steve's clothing. No evidence of blood, which would be surprising if he'd stabbed Jimmy. "I don't know, but I doubt it was Steve."

Mr. Franklin's back was to Steve, but Officer Drummond must've recognized him as he passed. Drummond instructed Annemarie's father to wait inside, then dashed after the other man.

Carol peered out the window after them. The sidewalk was well lit, but the parking lot beyond was eerily dark. What had happened to Jimmy out there? Moreover, what had provoked him to leave in the first place? Had he merely been afraid he'd be arrested if he stuck around until Officer Drummond came back?

Carol intercepted the officer the instant he returned. "What did Steve say?"

"He brought in a kid from the youth center with a dislocated shoulder," Drummond said. "Claims he was in the examining room with the boy the entire time, and the boy corroborates his story. I'll see if the nurses do too."

Drummond beckoned Marcy over. She confirmed Steve's story, then went into detail about Jimmy's disappearance. "He sneaked out of his curtained bed sometime between the time you left him and 10:44 pm," she told the officer.

"Do they know if Jimmy was stabbed in the hospital and then ran out, or if someone got to him after he went outside?" Drummond asked.

"Not yet," Marcy said. "If you'll excuse me, I need to get back to work."

Once Marcy left, Mr. Franklin stepped forward and peppered Officer Drummond with more questions.

Harvey pulled Carol aside. "Drummond is obviously going to have his hands full here for a while. We should go home and get some sleep so we can be of use to the search teams in the morning."

Carol agreed and relayed their plan to Bridget, who offered to meet them for the search as well.

During the drive home, Carol texted an update to Molly and Laura, telling them that unless new information came to light to redirect them elsewhere, she'd meet them at the corner of Rayburn Road and County Road 12 at dawn.

Harvey glanced at her screen while they were stopped at a red light. "Dawn will come mighty early," he warned her.

"We're always up that early," Carol reminded him. "At least it's Sunday, so we don't have to worry about opening the bakery."

"Small miracles," Harvey said.

"Mmhmm," Carol agreed as she gazed out into the inky night. *Now we just need a big one.*

The sun was already peeking over the horizon when Carol jumped out of bed the next morning to the aroma of pancakes and coffee. She found Harvey in the kitchen, carrying their breakfast plates to the table. "You should've woken me up."

"I figured you could use the extra few minutes of sleep. You've been going nonstop since Jeanette went missing."

Carol sat and savored a sip of coffee from the mug Harvey had set out for her. "Hopefully, today will change all that."

Harvey nodded. "I have a good feeling about it."

There wasn't a cloud in the sky as they drove to the rendezvous point, which made it easy to believe the search would have a positive outcome. Namely that they'd find Jeanette alive. Carol prayed they would, for Annemarie's sake. Jeanette always carried water and snacks with her when she hiked, so even though it had been four days since she was last seen, she could have survived this long—as long as her diabetes hadn't gotten the better of her.

By the time Carol and Harvey reached Rayburn Road, dozens of cars and several police cruisers lined both sides of the road. The deputy chief handed out maps to groups of searchers, who then piled into cars and drove off.

"Where are they going?" Carol asked Harvey. They caught up to Molly, Fergus, Hamish, and Laura, who were waiting their turn to speak to the deputy chief. "What's going on?"

"The police have divided the conservation area and surrounding undeveloped land into grids, and the deputy chief is assigning each group a section to search," Fergus explained. He was wearing a Loch Mallaig Volunteer Fire Company windbreaker, and Carol was glad someone with emergency training would be along on their search. "Some have to drive to other sections of the perimeter to start."

"I hope we can start here," Carol said. "According to Jimmy, this is where Jeanette's car was parked."

Fergus scratched his hand over his whiskery chin, looking contemplative.

"What?" Carol asked.

"It's nothing."

Carol winced. It occurred to her that if Jeanette had been kidnapped, her kidnapper might have abandoned her car here to throw searchers off her true trail. But then again, the guy Jimmy and Cedric ran into in the woods certainly sounded as if he'd had something to hide.

Carol glanced at a group of uniformed searchers receiving their assignment. "I see the Marquette search and rescue team brought a couple of dogs. Do you know if they told Annemarie to bring some of her mom's clothes for them to sniff?"

Laura squirmed and murmured, "They're actually cadaver dogs."

Carol's heart dropped. "Please don't tell Annemarie that."

"Tell me what?" Annemarie strode toward them with Mr. Franklin and Bridget flanking her. Scout lay nestled in Annemarie's arms, a leash clipped to his collar.

Carol felt her face heat as she anxiously searched her mind for something to say.

"The police cautioned us that we could be in for a long day," Fergus said smoothly, and Carol hoped Annemarie would believe him.

"Better that than giving up, right?" Bridget chirped.

"Aye," Hamish agreed as the others nodded.

The deputy police chief joined them. "Okay, your group can start from here. Fan out and walk abreast, leaving several feet between you. Officer Murdoch and Fergus will anchor either end of your chain to keep you in your grid. Got it?"

Everyone voiced assent, then followed Gillespie's instructions. As they approached the woods, Scout grew excited and strained to jump from Annemarie's arms.

"You know she's here, don't you?" Annemarie said to the dog. "Can you lead us to her?" Scout jerked in her arms, but she managed to stop him from leaping away. "Your leg can't handle walking yet. You're going to have to tell me where to go, okay?"

Annemarie's father turned to the deputy chief. "Since Scout seems to know where to go, shouldn't we follow his lead, rather than confine him to a grid?"

Gillespie studied the dog. "Okay, Mr. Franklin. You, Annemarie, Officer Anderson, and the dog can go on ahead and follow his lead. Greer will radio us if you find any sign of our missing person." He motioned Officer Greer Anderson over and directed her to accompany the pair and Scout.

Annemarie started out walking the trail, but she hadn't gone far before Scout began whining. "What is it, boy? Am I going the wrong way?" She turned toward the trees to her right. "Do you want me to go this way?"

The dog whined again.

Annemarie turned to her left. "This way?"

Scout attempted to lunge from her arms.

"This way it is then." They soon disappeared through the trees, although their voices could be heard calling "Mom" and "Jeanette" followed by the occasional yip from Scout.

An hour later, Carol's group reached the end of their grid with little to show for it. They'd found discarded food wrappers, but no evidence any of them had belonged to Jeanette.

"Hey," Bridget called to Annemarie, spotting her once more through the trees. "See anything?"

Annemarie and Mr. Franklin, who now carried Scout, trudged through the brambles to join them. "No," she replied. "I wish Scout could put weight on his leg already. Because a few times he seemed especially agitated, like the spot was significant, but we couldn't find any evidence why."

Officer Anderson consulted with Officer Murdoch about where to search next.

"Would you like me to carry Scout for a while?" Fergus volunteered. "Your arms must be getting tired."

Mr. Franklin looked to Annemarie. "Okay with you?"

At her nod, Fergus let Scout sniff his hand, then lifted the spaniel into his arms. He murmured, "Hey, buddy. Good boy. Let's find your mom, huh?" into the dog's ear, then started to walk, zigzagging in various directions based on the dog's reactions.

Suddenly Scout jumped from Fergus's arms and landed with a pained yelp before he dashed off, his leash trailing behind him.

Fergus lunged after him, only managing to swoop up air. "I'm so sorry. He's quick despite the bum leg." Fergus chased after Scout, and the rest of the search group followed.

"Hey, what's going on?" Officer Murdoch shouted.

"The dog's picked up a trail," Officer Anderson replied, then sprinted after Scout, her blonde ponytail bobbing. She soon passed half the group in her efforts to keep up with the dog.

As they rushed forward, Laura grinned at Carol, hope gleaming in her eyes. Her optimism injected a surge of energy into Carol's legs.

But just as it appeared no one would be able to catch him, Scout suddenly stopped. Soon, everyone was gathered around the dog.

"What is it?" Carol asked when she caught up.

Laura pointed to where Scout was belly crawling toward the edge of a hole surrounded by a smattering of broken, rotted boards. Carol thought they resembled the kind of wood that would've given Scout the splinter the vet found in his paw.

Officer Drummond pulled a flashlight from his utility belt. "It looks like an abandoned well."

"And from the condition of the trodden down path around the hole," Officer Anderson added, "the dog paced around it a fair bit before finding his way out of the woods."

Annemarie dropped to her knees at the dog's side. She rubbed the scruff around his neck as she peered eagerly over the edge. "Mom? Can you hear me?"

The hole seemed to swallow the light of Drummond's flashlight. He traced it down one side of the well, then the other.

"Stop," Mr. Franklin said sharply. "What was that?"

Drummond backed the light up a few inches.

"Mom! Mom!" Annemarie screamed, tears streaming down her face. "I see Mom!"

Carol caught the girl in her arms and gently pulled her back from the edge. "You've got to give the rescuers room to work. Okay, sweetie?"

Officer Anderson was already on her radio, relaying their coordinates to the captain of the Marquette search and rescue team and what equipment they needed.

Mr. Franklin teetered at the opening of the well. "Jeanette, honey? We're here. Talk to me." He stumbled, and dirt thudded down the hole.

Officer Drummond caught him by the arm and coaxed him to step back. "We don't want to cause a collapse. Don't worry. The rescue team will be here soon with ropes and pulleys, and we'll get your wife out of there."

"Did you hear that, Jeanette?" the businessman called down the hole in a watery voice. "We're going to get you out."

"Mom! Mom!" Annemarie continued to call until her voice broke and she burst into frantic sobs.

Jeanette wasn't answering her daughter's cries.

18

Officer Anderson put her radio away and coaxed Scout from the edge of the hole. She secured him to a tree. "You did a great job, boy. Now you need to let us do ours."

Annemarie's father took Carol's place holding his daughter while they all waited for the rest of the rescue team to arrive with the needed equipment.

Laura, Carol, and Molly congregated a few yards from the well. "It looks as if it was a simple accident," Laura said quietly. "We sure can let our imaginations get carried away with us."

"Was it an accident?" Carol scanned the small clearing, now too trodden down by searchers to tell if Jeanette had been *helped* into the abandoned well. "Or is that what someone wanted it to look like?"

"I see what you're saying," Molly said. "Then again, it's possible Jimmy made up the story about someone chasing him and his friend out of the woods and then running them down in the car."

Carol arched an eyebrow. "Not likely, given the bullet wound to his shoulder."

"Hmm," Laura said. "They could've run into somebody doing something illegal in the woods, like dealing drugs."

"Except the reason they went wandering through the woods in the first place was because they heard a dog yelping," Carol reminded her. Had the "nutcase" Jimmy described pushed Jeanette in or merely found her and left her to die, perhaps because he feared she had also seen something he didn't want her to?

"I guess we'll know as soon as Jeanette regains consciousness," Laura said, optimistically.

Carol's chest squeezed. "Yes," she managed to whisper, willing herself to believe Jeanette was still alive down there.

Two ATVs loaded with equipment and uniformed search team members sped to the scene. In no time, they had ropes rigged up and were lowering a petite member of the team down the hole, a light affixed to her hard hat.

Carol held her breath as they waited for her to reach Jeanette. Harvey squeezed Carol's hand and tears sprang to her eyes.

"She's alive!" the woman shouted, and cheers immediately erupted all around them.

The woman managed to secure the rope to Jeanette and maneuver the still-unconscious woman up past her so that she could steady her from below. Muscles strained and faces grimaced as the search team worked the ropes slowly upward.

When Mr. Franklin seemed ready to spring toward the hole the instant his wife appeared, Officer Anderson gripped his arm. "You need to let the paramedics do their job," she said firmly. "Your wife's medical care is our first priority. You understand?"

With a nod, Mr. Franklin settled for edging slightly closer to the action.

A moment later, Jeanette emerged from the hole, her neck secured in a spine-stabilizing collar. The petite woman who'd handled the mechanics of her extraction scrambled out behind her. Paramedics quickly strapped Jeanette to a spinal board and began taking vitals.

Once Jeanette was hooked up to an IV to help rehydrate her and declared stable enough for transport, Annemarie and her father were finally allowed to hold her hands.

"We're here, Mom," Annemarie said through tears. "You're going to be okay. Scout showed us where to find you. You picked a smart dog. We're going to have to give him a big treat for this."

Father and daughter both babbled away, talking about nothing in particular, except how scared they'd been when she hadn't come home, and glaringly omitting how frightened they obviously still were by her unresponsiveness.

At a questioning look from Mr. Franklin, one of the paramedics said, "Her vitals are okay, but it could take some time for her to regain consciousness. She's endured a harrowing few days."

Mr. Franklin swallowed hard, blinking back tears, and nodded.

He certainly didn't appear to be acting, but Carol supposed they'd have to wait a while longer before the police could ask her how she ended up in the abandoned well.

By the time Carol and her friends reached the trailhead, the ambulance had already left with Jeanette and her family—minus Scout, who was going home with Bridget—but many of the searchers continued to mill about, and a few news crews had arrived. Some of the volunteers must have heard the news and driven back from their outlying search areas because more cars were parked on the road now. Folks wore wide grins and slapped each other on the back, chatting animatedly.

Laura beamed at Carol. "I knew we'd find her."

Carol noticed a pair of officers heading back into the woods, carrying police tape, cameras, and other paraphernalia. "Apparently they're treating the area as a crime scene."

"I imagine they need to preserve whatever evidence might be left after all our tromping around in there," Molly said. "In case it wasn't an accident."

A TV reporter motioned her cameraman to turn his lens on the trio. "We understand you three recruited most of the searchers out here today and were present when the victim was located."

"We're grateful to be part of such a caring, close-knit community that is willing to do whatever it takes to help a neighbor in need," Carol said. "And we praise God for restoring our friend back to us."

More reporters had shoved their microphones toward Carol as she spoke, and the instant she finished, they erupted in an unintelligible cacophony of additional questions.

"We have no further comment," Hamish said sternly. When the reporters seemed as if they would press their luck, he gave a scowl that convinced them to round out their stories elsewhere.

"Would you all care to join me back at Castleglen for a celebratory luncheon?" Fergus asked the bakehouse group.

Molly turned hopeful eyes on Laura and Carol, but Harvey and Hamish were the first to cast their assenting votes. The ladies laughed, and Molly said, "I guess it's unanimous."

As they walked to their cars, Molly caught Laura and Carol by their arms and jutted her chin toward a cyclist mounting his bike. "Isn't that Steve?"

Carol cocked her head for a better view of his face, which was partially obscured by his helmet. "I think it is."

"Do you suppose he came to help search?" Molly asked.

"It wouldn't be the first time," Carol reminded her, mentally downplaying the fact that his company would fare better if Jeanette didn't regain consciousness before her husband's business sale deadline.

"What do you think Doreen's brother is doing here?" Hamish pointed to a man in a light-gray, double-breasted suit climbing out of a sleek Jaguar up the street.

Doreen still hadn't returned from her impromptu vacation either, and Carol didn't know which was more suspicious—her brother's presence or Doreen's absence.

Had he just been passing by on his way home from church and stopped out of curiosity? Or had he heard about Jeanette's rescue and was anxious to know what else the police might've discovered about her disappearance?

"The PI Mr. Franklin hired said he acted really cagey when questioned," Bridget piped up.

"Cagey how?" Fergus asked.

"Like not very . . ." Bridget's gaze shifted skyward as if she were searching for the perfect descriptor. "Forthcoming," she finally said. "The PI said he wasn't very forthcoming."

Carol couldn't blame him. The PI had struck her as a bit slippery himself, but the news did make her extra anxious to hear Jeanette's story of what had really happened.

Half an hour later, they'd all settled around a large table on the outdoor terrace overlooking Castleglen's eighteenth green so that Scout—their hero of the day—could join them. Fergus slipped inside for a few minutes, then emerged with a chew toy shaped like a golf bag, likely from the gift shop, for the dog to gnaw on.

As for the rest of their little group, they enjoyed club sandwiches prepared on sourdough from Bread on Arrival and homemade kettle chips from Tee for Two, the resort's casual bistro. Thanks to the delicious lunch and carefree conversation, Carol realized the tension that had been twisting her gut for the past few days had finally released its hold.

Whatever had happened, Jeanette was now safe.

Carol was just contemplating ordering a Bread on Arrival brownie for dessert when Bridget sprang to her feet, waving her phone. "Annemarie texted. Jeanette is awake. And she wants to see us."

Excitement welled in Carol's chest. They'd finally have their answers. She glanced at Harvey.

"You go with your friends," he said. "I'll take care of Scout at the house, and Bridget can pick him up when she brings you back."

"I think Jeanette might want to see her dog too," Molly said. "I know I would if Angus had saved my life like that. I'm not sure how the hospital staff would react though." She pulled out her phone. "I'll call and ask."

Ten minutes later, with Scout's visiting privileges approved, Carol and her friends headed to the hospital. Annemarie met them in the hallway and lifted Scout into her arms. "Officer Drummond just arrived to ask Mom some questions, but I convinced him to let you join us since you all were instrumental in helping us find her."

"Are you sure?" Laura asked. "We don't want to overwhelm her after all she's been through."

Scout licked Annemarie's face, earning himself a snuggle. "I'm sure," she said brightly.

They tiptoed into the room behind Annemarie so Jeanette could greet her beloved hero first. Scout's tail whipped back and forth like a rocket the instant he glimpsed his mistress.

"How's my boy?" Jeanette reached out to draw him onto the bed beside her.

"Watch your IV," her husband cautioned, catching it a second before the dog would have tangled his legs in the long tubing.

The dog's entire rear end wagged with elation as he lathered Jeanette's face with slobbery kisses.

"I love you too, boy. You did good." Jeanette scratched behind Scout's ears until he finally laid down at her side and rested his head on her midsection. Then she turned her attention to Bridget, Molly, Laura, and Carol. "Annemarie tells me I also have you wonderful ladies to thank for finding me."

"We were happy to help," Carol said as the others voiced similar agreement.

Officer Drummond cleared his throat. "Before you tire yourself out with all these thank-yous, could I ask you a few questions for my report?"

Jeanette sighed. "Certainly."

The officer set out a small recording device on the bedside table. "For starters, how did you end up in the well?"

"That was my own fault. I stumbled into it."

Carol exchanged glances with Molly and Laura. She didn't know about them, but somehow after all their theorizing the truth felt a little anticlimactic to her.

"No one pushed you?" Officer Drummond clarified.

"No, but someone did find me and ignore my cries for help. Well, he said he was fetching help, but he never came back." She frowned. "At least, I don't think he did. No, that's not right either. He did come back later, but then left again."

"Why were you hiking so far off the trail in the first place?" Mr. Franklin interjected, his tone mild but infused with concern. "And why weren't you parked at a trailhead?"

Jeanette ducked her head sheepishly. "The Kleins were texting me about borrowing the boat that morning, so I pulled over on the side of the road to tell them it was fine. I thought I could cut through to a trail from there, so I just left the car. Out of nowhere, Scout took off after a rabbit and wasn't responding to my whistles, so I raced after him. He disappeared into an old barn and when—"

"Excuse me," Officer Drummond interrupted. "This old barn . . . where was it relative to the well?"

Jeanette's face scrunched in concentration as she considered the question. "I'm not sure. When I followed Scout into the barn, a man wielding a branding iron turned on him." She buried her fingers in Scout's fur. "He thrust the iron dangerously close to Scout and ordered him out."

Mr. Franklin squeezed his wife's hand and she momentarily fell silent, studying their interlocked fingers.

"Did you recognize the man?" Officer Drummond prompted.

Jeanette shrugged. "I don't think so. It all happened so fast. And what little light was slanting through the barn boards just seemed to bounce off the dust in the air. All I was thinking was that we had to get out of there."

"Can you describe him?"

Jeanette's gaze shifted to the empty space beyond Drummond's left shoulder and she almost seemed to wince. No doubt conjuring up the man's image was the last thing she wanted to do.

"We'll come back to that," Drummond said gently. "Did the man see you?"

A cold shiver snaked down Carol's spine.

Jeanette shrank deeper under her bedcovers. "I'm not sure. I remember thinking my heart was pounding so hard he could probably hear it. But I'd panicked and ducked behind an old wagon. It shielded me from his line of sight, I think." She shifted her gaze to Scout. "I'm not sure he even heard me calling for Scout before that because he'd been hammering and clanging."

"So the dog ran back out of the barn?" Drummond asked.

"Yes, and I was right behind him," Jeanette said. "I don't know how far we ran before I crashed through the rotted boards covering the old well. I was watching behind me to make sure he wasn't following us, so I didn't even see the well."

"We didn't notice a barn in the immediate vicinity, but we'll find it," the officer told her. "Do you think this man you saw yell at Scout is the same one who failed to help you get out of the well?"

Jeanette expelled a heavy breath. "I'm not sure. At first I tried to climb out on my own, not wanting to attract his attention after how badly he'd scared me."

Scout whined, no doubt sensing the rising tension in his mistress.

"Maybe we should save the rest of your questions for after my wife's more rested," Mr. Franklin suggested.

"I'm okay." Jeanette extracted her hand from his grasp and buried it once again in Scout's fur.

Carol studied the dog. He didn't show a smidgen of animosity toward Jeanette's husband, so surely he couldn't have been the man Jimmy and Cedric encountered in the woods after they heard the dog yelp—a man who'd presumably left Jeanette for dead, killed Cedric, and attempted to kill Jimmy . . . twice.

"Scout circled the hole, barking frantically," Jeanette recounted. "Eventually the noise must've gotten to the man. He came out and ordered Scout away again. And I think he might've shot off a gun to try to scare him. I was petrified he shot Scout, but the next moment, instead of running away, Scout scratched at the boards as if to show the man what he needed to do. At that point, I yelled for help too."

"Did he look down the well?" Annemarie asked, her face white with tension as her mother told her story.

Jeanette nodded. "He pulled away more boards and asked if I was hurt."

"Can you describe what he looked like?" Officer Drummond asked.

"No. It was pitch-black in the hole and the sun was behind him. To be honest, at that moment, he looked like an angel to me. I explained how I'd been chasing my dog and apologized for his going into the barn. At that point, the man abruptly stopped tugging away the boards. He asked if I'd been in the barn too." She shuddered. "I think admitting I had been was my mistake. After that he was silent for a long time. Finally he said he needed to find some rope to pull me out. He said he'd call my family, but I told him nobody would answer. He promised he'd be back soon." Tears filled her eyes. "I don't remember a lot after that. I didn't have a watch, and my phone had fallen out of my pocket into the puddle of water at the bottom of the well, so I had no idea how much time passed. But the minutes seemed like hours."

"Oh Mom," Annemarie whispered.

Jeanette ruffled Scout's ears. "This little guy stayed at the top of the hole, whining. When daylight started to disappear, I concluded the man wasn't coming back or couldn't find me again. So I urged Scout to go for help."

"One person we talked to said she spotted him near the road," Carol said. "When she attempted to coax him into her car, he kept turning back toward the woods. In retrospect, she realized he was probably trying to get her to follow him."

"You ladies worked so hard to find me, didn't you?" Jeanette gave Carol a wan smile, fatigue clearly taxing her energy reserves. Despite exhaustion, she continued her story. "As the night wore on, I grew terrified I'd run out of food and that the doses of insulin I was carrying in my to-go kit wouldn't be enough. Annemarie wasn't due home for days"—Jeanette glanced lovingly at her daughter—"so I didn't think anyone would miss me until it was too late."

Mr. Franklin winced at the implications of her statement.

"Then the man suddenly reappeared," Jeanette went on. "He shined a flashlight down the hole and asked how I was doing. I was over the moon with joy. He had a rope, but then acted indecisive about how to proceed. I couldn't believe he hadn't called the rescue team hours before, but I didn't want to anger him by saying so. He walked around the hole muttering for what seemed like an eternity. Then Scout must have heard me pleading because he came back. He barked at the man, then yelped as if he'd been smacked."

Drummond nodded. It followed along with Jimmy's story.

"Then the man started yelling," Jeanette went on, "but not at me. It didn't sound as if he was talking to the dog either. The next thing I knew, he was gone. And he never came back. At least not that I remember. It's all kind of fuzzy after that."

"Would you recognize the man's voice if you heard it again?" Officer Drummond asked.

Jeanette shrugged.

"Was there anything distinctive about it? Inflections? An accent? Anything?"

She swiped at her damp eyes. "I'm afraid I was too focused on getting out to pay attention to that kind of detail."

A nurse bustled into Jeanette's room. After one glance at her patient, she dismissed the visitors. "She needs her rest. Any more questions will have to wait."

Officer Drummond clicked off the recorder. "If you think of anything else that might help us identify the man who left you, please call me."

"I will," Jeanette promised. "But honestly, I'd rather forget the whole thing."

Drummond grimaced, but said nothing and exited the room. Bridget and the Bakehouse Three followed, trailed by Mr. Franklin carrying Scout. Annemarie lingered in the hospital room.

As Mr. Franklin handed the dog back to Bridget, he fixed a laser gaze on Officer Drummond. "What didn't you say back there?"

A muscle in Drummond's jaw twitched. "I believe the young men who stole your wife's car are who she heard her would-be rescuer yelling at. And there's strong evidence that in addition to leaving your wife for dead, he killed one of the men and attempted to kill the other."

Mr. Franklin gaped at him. "The kid at the hospital last night?" He shot a panicked glance at the door to his wife's room. "Do you think he'd try to come after Jeanette?"

Drummond heaved a deep sigh. "It seems likely he thinks she can identify him or that she saw something he doesn't want her talking about. Otherwise, he could've anonymously called in her location days ago. So yes, it is possible he'd try to interfere."

"Probable, you mean," Mr. Franklin said, the waver in his voice all but begging Drummond to deny it.

But Officer Drummond didn't. "We'll assign a patroller to guard her room and alert hospital security."

Mr. Franklin sank to the floor, his back dragging against the wall on the way down. He clasped his head. "I can't lose her. Not again. Not when everything is finally coming together for us."

Annemarie stepped out of Jeanette's room. "Dad, what's wrong?"

Shaking his head, her dad swiped at his damp cheeks with his sleeve, but he didn't seem capable of articulating the reassurance he clearly wanted to give her.

Laura gave Annemarie a sideways hug. "He's just happy your mom is okay. The worry of the past few days has been overwhelming, and you know how strong men like to be for the women in their lives. It's just caught up to him now."

Annemarie stooped next to her father and hugged him fiercely. "Mom's going to be okay. You'll see. The doctor warned her she could have nightmares for a while and he's making an appointment for her to talk with a counselor. But she's going to need you to be there for her. Can you do that?"

Mr. Franklin stared into his daughter's face, and for the first time, Carol saw him not as a calculating businessman, but as a man who would do anything to restore his family. "I will. Whatever it takes, I will be there for her."

19

Carol, Laura, and Molly lingered in the hospital lobby as Officer Drummond gave instructions to the young patroller assigned to guard Jeanette.

Once the patroller finally headed to the elevator, Drummond shot a wary glance their way. "Do you have more information for me?" he asked, clearly indicating he didn't want them plying him for the same.

Molly ignored the implication. "Is there a barn in those woods? Because none of us noticed one."

"I didn't either." He wearily raked his fingers through his hair. "But I don't want you hunting for it. That's our job."

Laura frowned. "Don't you think it would have been within sight of the abandoned well if it really existed? Jeanette was trapped a long time. Maybe her mind pieced together the wild story from her nightmares."

Carol shook her head. "But she couldn't have made up the crazed man. Her story lines up exactly with what Jimmy said happened Wednesday night."

"And that crazed man is the reason you women need to stay away from this case," Officer Drummond said sternly.

"Will you arrest the guy?" Molly asked. "If you find him in the barn, I mean."

"If I can prove he was the one who left Jeanette to die or who attacked Cedric and Jimmy." He stifled a yawn and glanced longingly toward the coffee kiosk.

Poor guy. The officer was coming off a late night with Jimmy Walker, and he'd already had a long day. And given Jeanette's account, the day was still far from over. Because if he didn't find the barn and track down the man using it before the man found Jeanette—

"Don't worry," Officer Drummond broke into Carol's thoughts. "If there's a barn to be found out there, we'll find it."

The women each shook his hand in turn and thanked him. As they headed to the exit, Carol checked her watch. "Do you two want to join Harvey and me for dinner?"

"I never turn down a meal I don't have to cook," Molly said. "I guess you need a ride too, since Bridget's already left with Scout. Do you mind if we stop by my place and pick up Angus? He's been cooped up all day. And he loves racing around your big yard."

"Of course he can come." Carol smiled. "I've got a real soft spot for dogs today."

When they reached Carol's house, Angus didn't know where to run first. He raced toward the chicken coop and sniffed at the fence enthusiastically, then he sprinted to say hello to Harvey, who was relaxing in a rocking chair on the front porch. Harvey returned the joyful greeting with a vigorous head rub.

"Laura and Molly are joining us for dinner," Carol explained as she, Laura, and Molly climbed the porch steps. "I thought I'd pull a couple of my homemade pizzas from the freezer. Shouldn't take long to heat them up."

"You don't have to convince me," Harvey said, then stood and trailed the women into the house. "So how is Jeanette doing?"

While she preheated the oven and made a salad, Carol filled him in on all Jeanette had revealed about her ordeal. Once she'd shared everything, she asked, "Did you notice a barn when we were out there?"

"I didn't see it," Harvey said. "But there is one out there—if it's still standing."

Stunned by his certainty, Carol halted with her knife poised above a carrot and stared at him. "How do you know that?"

"Do you have that map?" he asked.

Carol set down her knife and retrieved the map from her purse. Harvey spread it on the table, and they all huddled around it.

Harvey traced the road parallel to Rayburn Road, where Jimmy had claimed they'd found Jeanette's car. "See this?" He pointed to a broken line designating an old logging road. "This borders the conservation area. And in here somewhere"—his finger circled an area part of the way up the road—"there used to be a driveway to the homestead that was on the property before it and all the surrounding farmland was donated to the town."

"But it's not farmland," Laura said.

"Not now." Harvey rocked back on his heels, relishing his role as storyteller. "But it was eighty years ago when the owner died. The town turned it into the McFarlane Conservation Area."

"How do you know all this?" Carol asked. Her husband had grown up in Pittsburgh, not Loch Mallaig.

"I majored in journalism, remember?"

Molly's face twisted in confusion. "And you investigated the old barn?"

Harvey chuckled. "Not exactly. When I was in college, the farmhouse burned down under suspicious circumstances purported to have connections to the son of a prominent state politician."

"Ah," Laura said. "When anything shady happens that's connected to some politician, you must know the press will jump on it."

"Even press in training," Harvey said with a chuckle. "I just happened to be college classmates with the son, so it was big news on campus. My editor at the Newkirk College newspaper sent me to cover the story."

"Oh, I remember that now," Carol chimed in. "You told me about it on our first date. The politician's son and some buddies were partying in the abandoned old place when it caught fire."

Harvey nodded. "They claimed they were just exploring, and I suspect some pressure from the higher-ups convinced the fire marshal not to try too hard to find evidence to the contrary. Anyway, the fire never reached the barn, so it's possible it's still standing."

Molly studied the map. "But if Jeanette was parked here, how'd she wind up way over there?" She pointed out the different areas. "And how did the boys happen upon her car?" She traced another line. "You'd think they would've picked up this trail."

Harvey shook his head. "It was dark, so they didn't likely know which way they were headed. My guess is that Jimmy and Cedric ran toward the glow of the greenhouses further down on Rayburn. It was probably the only light they could see."

"That makes sense," Laura agreed.

"And Scout chasing the rabbit explains why Jeanette wound up so far off the trail," Molly added. "It's not nearly as far away if you cut straight through the woods rather than follow the hiking trail."

"And as I recall," Harvey said, "the old hip-roofed barn belonging to the homestead was quite a distance from the house that burned down."

"I should call Officer Drummond to let him know," Carol said, pulling out her cell phone. After three rings went unanswered, she mentally rehearsed the message she should leave, but the connection clicked off without going to voice mail. Carol frowned at her phone. "I think he just hung up on me."

"I'm sure it wasn't on purpose," Laura said. "Why don't you text him the info?"

Carol dashed off a text, and his response was almost immediate. *Thanks for the tip. We'll scout it.*

"I wouldn't mind going and checking out the place too." Harvey's eyes sparked. "I could probably freelance another investigative piece out of the story."

"The police don't want us getting on that crazy guy's radar," Laura reminded him.

Harvey swatted away the protest with a flap of his hand. "If he had something to hide, I'm sure he's long since cleared out whatever it was, especially after running into three people out there in one evening. And if he hasn't, I doubt he'd risk venturing back until he's sure the cops aren't there."

Molly scrunched her nose as she studied the map. "Isn't that the logging road we saw Henry Roberts's truck coming out of yesterday afternoon? None of our vehicles could traverse those ruts and overgrown brambles."

"I bet Devin would lend us his ATV again," Harvey said, taking his phone out of his pocket.

But Carol's mind had stalled on Henry's name. Could the old barn be where he met an illicit supplier? Granted, they had no reason to suspect him of dealing in stolen goods other than Doreen's allegations. Except why else would he be on an old logging road in the middle of nowhere?

By the time they finished eating and drove out to the old logging road, Devin was already there with his ATV, which was loaded onto a trailer attached to a red pickup. Carol assessed the four-seater and grimaced. One of them would have to walk.

Devin handed the keys to Harvey. "You comfortable driving?"

"Are you sure you don't mind?" Harvey asked.

"Nah, that's why I brought it on a trailer this time," Devin said. "You can call when you're heading in again, and I'll meet you back here to load her up."

Harvey set out for the barn at a steady clip, but when two parked ATVs came into view, he slowed.

"Those belong to the police department," Carol said, recognizing the logo on the back.

Officer Drummond must have heard the sound of their vehicle approaching. By the time the barn came into view, he stood at the door, scowling at them.

As Harvey shut off the ignition, Drummond asked wryly, "What part of 'don't look for the barn' didn't I make clear?"

"It's my fault," Harvey said. "I wrote a piece on an arson here years ago. And the investigative reporter in me couldn't resist checking into what secrets the place still held."

The officer frowned. "I'm afraid you made the trip for nothing. We can't allow you in until we're ready to release the scene."

"Could you at least tell us if you've figured out what the guy was so seemingly desperate to keep secret?" Laura asked.

Drummond shrugged. "Not really. There's nothing but a bunch of old furniture in there. Now if you'll excuse me . . ." He headed back into the barn.

"Wait," Carol blurted. "Old as in antique?"

Drummond snorted. "If you scrub off a hundred years of accumulated dust maybe. The farmer who originally willed this place to the county for a conservation area must've leased space out for storage or something after he gave up farming."

"No," Harvey interjected. "The last owner of the property wasn't a farmer. He was the farmer's son, Paul McFarlane. He never married or had children, which is why he left the property to the townspeople."

"So the son leased out space," Drummond said impatiently.

"No," Harvey corrected. "The son was a renowned furniture maker, an apprentice of Gustav Stickley. Paul moved back to Loch Mallaig after old man McFarlane passed."

Molly gasped. "Yesterday afternoon, we saw Henry Roberts drive out of the dead-end road this driveway intersects."

Drummond's expression was pinched. "Henry Roberts? The senior citizen who runs that antiques shop?"

"And who had Scout's dog tag in his pocket," Carol reminded him. "I bet it fell off in the barn or near the well and Henry picked it up."

"And from the sounds of what you found in the barn," Molly chimed in, "he's been looting the furniture this long-dead craftsman made and passing it off as authentic Scottish antiques."

Harvey shook his head. "Or the old man could've bought the furniture from some shyster who convinced him the pieces were authentic."

Laura sighed. "It would explain why Jeanette didn't seem to recognize the man she saw in the barn. If he was some kind of middleman, I mean. She's shopped in Henry's store—she probably owns at least one piece of this furniture even—so you'd think she would've recognized him."

"Although..." Carol frowned, unconvinced. "Sometimes you don't recognize people you know when they're in a different environment than the one you normally see them in. I've had students who'd spent a year or two in my math classes but barely recognized me when we ran into each other at the grocery store."

"Besides," Molly added, "Jeanette was scared. I give her a pass for not recognizing someone she only met once or twice."

Officer Anderson stepped out of the barn carrying a slab of

barn board. "Look what we found behind that old forge," she said to Drummond. "I'm thinking the branding iron Mrs. Franklin mentioned could've been used to make this." She turned the wood around to show a burned impression that read *Made in Scotland 1908*.

Carol gasped. "Roberts sold Jeanette a table with that burned into the underside. Talk to Annemarie and ask her to show you the table. I'm positive you'll find it's an exact match." Carol shivered at what else that likely meant.

Henry Roberts was a murderer.

Butterflies danced in Carol's stomach as she arrived at the bakery extra early Monday morning to bake a fresh batch of oatcakes for Jeanette, who remained at the hospital. She had run out of food and insulin after two days, so she was still weak and recovering under a doctor's care.

Carol hadn't heard anything more from Officer Drummond since leaving him at the barn the night before, and she was anxious about any further findings. Despite the evidence pointing to Henry Roberts, Drummond had said it wasn't enough to convince a judge to sign a search warrant for the man's home and business. Like Harvey had said, Mr. Roberts could have bought the coffee table he sold Jeanette from a middleman.

An urgent rapping sounded at the back door, so Carol hurried to answer it. On the stoop stood Doreen in a blindingly yellow sundress, and the redhead appeared quite impatient.

"Did you hear the news?" Doreen exclaimed.

Carol's butterflies swooped into her throat. Was she talking about Henry Roberts?

Laura emerged from the kitchen carrying a tray of scones and stopped short, sending the baked goods sliding to one end of the tray. "Where have you been all weekend?" she scolded Doreen.

Doreen grinned. "I was doing a little sleuthing of my own. I spent the weekend scouring the historical archives in the biggest library in the Upper Peninsula."

Carol sighed. That explained why she'd had her phone off and her brother's calls hadn't gone through.

Molly hurried down the stairs from her second story apartment, Angus at her heels.

"And you'll never guess what I found," Doreen went on.

"What?" Molly asked.

"Photographic proof Henry Roberts is committing fraud!" Doreen paused for dramatic effect, then rushed on. "And completely boneheaded fraud at that. Several pieces of furniture he is displaying in his shop and trying to pass off as antique Scottish imports—which of course makes them all the more attractive to tourists—were really built right here in Loch Mallaig by a famous craftsman a hundred years ago." She rolled her eyes. "Apparently he doesn't know that they'd be worth three times as much if he was selling them as the real deal: Paul McFarlane originals."

"Did you give the photographs to Officer Drummond?" Laura asked.

"That might be just what he needs to secure a search warrant so they can find evidence to connect him to the murder," Carol added.

Doreen's eyes widened. "Henry murdered someone?"

Carol bit her lip, annoyed at herself for letting her thoughts spill out—especially to someone who liked to disseminate information as gleefully as Doreen.

"Well?" Doreen's voice hit an octave Carol hadn't heard before. "You can't leave me hanging."

"You said *you* had news," Carol reminded her, hoping to determine what she did and didn't already know before giving her any more fodder. "Did you find anything other than the photos?"

Doreen's voice slipped into a conspiratorial tone. "I did go to the police station first thing this morning with copies of the photographs and overheard them talking about needing more proof to write up a warrant." She beamed with pride. "And after Officer Drummond saw my pictures, he said they were perfect. When I left, one of the officers was going to have a judge sign the warrant."

Relief swept over Carol. With any luck, they'd find the gun Jimmy claimed Cedric's murderer had used, and anything that might definitively connect Henry to Jimmy's attempted murder at the hospital and to Jeanette.

Carol sighed. As happy as she was to hear the police were securing a search warrant for Henry's place, she hoped he wasn't the man who had left Jeanette for dead. It would be a lot less upsetting if he'd merely been unwittingly buying the furniture from a criminal, especially if he could give up the creep's name and location.

"If you're going to get those oatcakes to Jeanette before the bakery opens, you'd better get them in the oven," Laura reminded Carol, putting an end to her mental gymnastics, and thankfully relieving her from having to explain to Doreen what she'd meant about connecting Henry Roberts to a murder.

An hour later, the junior officer standing outside Jeanette's hospital room door gazed longingly at the bakery box Carol carried. "Whatever is in there smells fantastic," he said.

"Oatcakes," she said with a grin. When his face fell, she added, "And some blueberry streusel muffins." She opened the box. "Help yourself. There are plenty."

The young man reached in and gingerly removed a giant muffin from the box. "The doctor is in with Mrs. Franklin now." He lowered his voice to a whisper. "Her husband asked that visitors don't tell her I'm standing guard out here. He doesn't want to worry her."

"I understand." Carol glanced at her watch and peeked around the door.

Jeanette appeared to be asleep. The doctor, wearing light green scrubs and skull cap as if he'd just come out of surgery, stood on the other side of her bed, examining her IV. He pulled a hypodermic needle from his pants pocket and inserted into a port.

Carol blinked. *Doctors don't carry needles in their pockets.* Confusion melted away in an instant when, with sickening clarity, it hit her.

That was no doctor.

20

Carol rushed into the room. "Hey! What are you doing?"

The doctor pushed the plunger on the needle and an air bubble skittered down the IV line.

Time seemed to slow for Carol as she remembered reading that if an air bubble was injected into a person's veins, it would stop the blood flow, and the person could die. She couldn't let that happen.

Dropping the box of muffins, Carol lunged toward the bed and yanked the tube from Jeanette's arm just before the bubble would have reached her vein.

Alerted by the commotion, the officer outside the door raced into the room, and the fake doctor grabbed Carol as a human shield.

He held the hypodermic to the side of her neck. "Back away or she dies," the man said, his voice low and sinister, yet familiar.

"Henry?" Carol twisted her head to try and see his face, but the needle poked her skin.

"Sir," the officer said calmly, "let go of the woman and put the needle down."

Out of the corner of her eye, Carol noticed Jeanette's hand inch toward her call button. Jeanette's eyes stayed closed, as if she were pretending to be asleep.

Henry tightened his hold on Carol. "I'm too old to go back to jail."

Back to jail? So Doreen had been right about him from the beginning. Carol stretched her neck away from the needle as she struggled to break free of his firm grip.

Carol turned fearful eyes on the officer. His gun was aimed at Henry, but a few inches off and a bullet would hit her instead. She prayed he wouldn't attempt a shot before she could duck.

"You can't get away with this," she said, stalling. "The police already found the barn full of furniture and the branding iron." She remembered how squeaky clean the exterior of his truck had been when they dropped by on Thursday. Trying to get rid of the evidence he'd rammed Jeanette's stolen Saab? "They've probably already found marks on your truck from where you hit Jeanette's car when you were chasing those kids."

The man's sharp intake of breath confirmed her theory. And that he clearly hadn't expected the police to connect him to Jimmy and Cedric.

"It's only a matter of time before they find the weapon you used on them, if they haven't already." Carol hoped that if she could distract Henry with chatter, the officer could take him down. "Is this how you got to Jimmy in the hospital? How did you know he was there? What were you doing? Listening to a police scanner?"

"Shut up!" Henry shoved her forward a step, pasting himself behind her. "Drop the gun, cop. I've got nothing to lose."

Carol's heart thumped.

The young officer seemed to waver.

"No!" Jeanette yelled, rolling off the other side of the bed.

Carol jabbed her elbow into Henry's gut and dropped like a rock to twist out of his grip.

The officer's gun went off, and the window behind them shattered.

Carol scrambled to her knees and flipped off the wheel lock on Jeanette's bed. Henry lurched for the door, but Carol grabbed Jeanette's bed rails and shoved the bed at Henry, pinning him to the wall.

Officer Drummond raced into the room, his gaze skittering from Jeanette gripping a coatrack over her head like a weapon to the bed pinning Henry to the wall to the other officer pointing his gun at Henry and shouting at him to raise his hands.

Drummond yanked handcuffs from his utility belt and clapped them on Roberts's wrists. "Henry Roberts, you're under arrest for the murder of Cedric Button."

"And the attempted murder of Jimmy Walker," Carol piped up.

"And me," Jeanette added.

"Not to mention for fraud." Carol looked at Drummond. "Did you find the gun he used on Jimmy?"

Drummond shoved the now handcuffed Henry toward the other officer. "Take him to the station and book him." After the younger officer left the room with Henry, Drummond said, "We found the gun, and a knife. I have no doubt it'll match the description of the weapon the doctor said would have been used to stab Jimmy." He helped Jeanette to her feet. "Are you okay?"

"I am now, thanks to Carol." Jeanette shot her a shaky smile.

"Henry pushed an air bubble into her IV," Carol explained. "If I'd been a second later . . ."

Jack Franklin's voice rose from the hallway. "That's my wife in there. Let me pass!"

Drummond stuck his head out the door and spoke to a new officer standing sentry. "It's okay. He can come in."

He rushed into the room and swept Jeanette into his arms, anxiously examining her face. "Are you okay? He didn't hurt you?"

Tears trickled down Jeanette's cheeks as she hugged her husband. "I'm wonderful."

Over her head, Mr. Franklin said hoarsely to Carol, "You've saved my wife. Again. How can I ever repay you?"

"No reward necessary, Mr. Franklin," Carol told him with a smile.

He actually smiled back. "Please. Call me Jack."

---❈---

By the following Thursday, everyone in Loch Mallaig seemed to know what had happened to Jeanette, Jimmy Walker, and Cedric Button. It remained the hot topic of conversation for Bread on Arrival's customers, who continued pouring in to gossip over the news of Henry Roberts's arrest.

During a particularly busy midday rush that had Carol, Hamish, and Molly all hustling to help customers, Angus raced down the stairs from Molly's apartment and let out a joyous yip. He ran to the front windows and pawed at the glass.

"What's gotten into you?" Carol asked, wondering when Hamish would have time to fix Molly's door.

When she reached the window, however, she smiled when she realized what had Angus so excited. Scout, panting blithely, was on the other side of the glass, accompanied by all three Franklins.

Carol hurried to the door and ushered Jeanette, Jack, and Annemarie inside. "Bring Scout too," she said. "We can make a health-code exception for a hero."

When the family entered, the other customers broke into thunderous applause, and Jeanette blushed. "Thank you all." She warmly looked from one person to the next. "I know many of you participated in the searches for me. I feel so blessed to have such a wonderful community watching out for my welfare."

Hamish, who was filling a coffee cup for his current customer, lifted the mug in salute. "Och, we're just glad you're all right, lass."

"Not just all right." Jeanette smiled as she slipped her hand into Jack's. He beamed at her. "Better than ever."

"We have a lot to celebrate," Jack said as he patiently untangled himself from Scout's leash while the spaniel and Angus eagerly greeted each other. "In fact, we're headed to Neeps and Tatties for a celebratory lunch with Glenn Giobsan and Steve Gambel right now."

"Steve?" Carol squeaked. Did Jack know that Jeanette had been communicating with him online?

As if reading Carol's thoughts, Annemarie sidled up to her. "Mom thought Puppy Love was a meetup site for *dogs*," the girl murmured behind her hand. "She had no idea that Steve was interested in her romantically. She just thought she was making Scout a new friend."

"Oh my," Carol said. "I feel bad for Steve, though."

"Don't feel bad." Annemarie giggled. "I saw him visit Jimmy Walker in the hospital yesterday. When I wheeled Mom out after her discharge, he was chatting with that hospital receptionist, Marcy. I think he's moved on."

"Glad to hear it," Carol said, then returned her attention to Jack. "So you're celebrating. Has your business deal gone through, then?"

Jack and Jeanette exchanged glances. "There's a new deal on the table," Jeanette said. "Instead of being bought out by a massive corporation, Jack is partnering up with Steve and Glenn so their three businesses can compete with the big guy together."

"Yes, but I'll be a *silent* partner." Jack kissed his wife's forehead. "No more late nights."

"Maybe some early mornings on the trail, though." Jeanette grinned up at her husband, then said to Carol, "We're here for my oatcakes. Jack and I are going hiking tomorrow."

"Wonderful," Carol said. Noticing that the customer line had emptied, she ushered the Franklins toward the counter. "I'll fill a box for you now."

As Carol boxed oatcakes, Jeanette glanced around the café area. Her gaze stopped when it reached the fireplace, where a cherry accent table now rested. "Is that . . . ?"

Carol nodded. "A McFarlane original, but without the forged Scotland brand. The mayor delivered it himself last night in thanks for our help in uncovering the barn full of McFarlane furniture."

"You deserve it and so much more," Jeanette said. "I gave up mine for evidence and told them to keep it."

"Good riddance to that reminder," Jack put in.

"What are they doing with the rest of the furniture?" Annemarie asked. "I heard it's worth a lot since the guy who made it was famous."

"There's some debate," Carol said. "But it sounds like they'll put some on display at town hall, then auction off the rest of it to support local charities."

"I'm glad good is coming out of Henry Roberts's scheme." Jack handed over money for the oatcakes.

Carol rang up the sale, then gave Jeanette the package. "I'll have these boxed and ready for you again next week."

"Better add another dozen," Jack said. "I'm acquiring a taste for them myself."

As she watched the reunited family depart, laughing and joking as they went, Carol felt a surge of pride. She'd wanted to go into the bakery business partly because she knew that baked goods made people happy. What she hadn't realized were all the unexpected ways this middle-age adventure would enrich her own life as well.

Up to this point, we've been doing all the writing. Now it's *your* turn!

Tell us what you think about this book, the characters, the bad guy, or anything else you'd like to share with us about this series. We can't wait to hear from *you*!

Log on to give us your feedback at:
https://www.surveymonkey.com/r/ScottishBakehouse

Annie's FICTION